TEARS OF KERBEROS

First published in the United Kingdom in May 2011
This Second Edition published August 2011
by Swordworks Books.

ISBN 978-1906512309

Typeset by Swordworks Books
Printed and bound in the UK & US
A catalogue record of this book is available
from the British Library

Cover design by Swordworks Books
www.swordworks.co.uk

TEARS OF KERBEROS

MICHAEL G. THOMAS

CHAPTER ONE

The first victory for the Centauri Confederacy was the bloody and costly Siege of Titan. Though the Zealots and their supporters had been pushed out, the revolt on the planet below had taken a violent and terrifying turn for the worse. Throughout the Confederacy the ships and people of the Confederate Military mobilised and prepared for the coming storm, the war that would move from an insurgency to the bloodiest conflict since the Great War.

Reports of the Proxima Emergency

Spartan should have been resting. It was four days since the events on board the Titan Naval Station and his wounds had barely healed. He was still covered in bruises and the stitches on his arm could do with another week of healing. Since returning to the Fleet he had been suffering from recurring headaches, apparently a common symptom of prolonged combat in close environments. It didn't matter though, events had changed and taking a break was for somebody else right now. The insurgency down on the planet of Prime had taken over most of the Northern colony of Avagana and the other six colonies were experiencing a variety of suicide attacks and hijackings. What had started as a violent insurgency against the state was quickly starting to look like the first stages of civil war. Spartan wasn't a career soldier by any means. His life just a year ago had been completely different. He was a well-built man but unfortunately a series of poor decisions had resulted in him fighting in the underground pit fighter circuit. The fights were illegal in the Confederacy but the money was good and he needed the cash to pay of his substantial debts. A bungled police raid had left him with a dead police officer at his feet and a choice between the military or prison. With the insurgency moving fast he was already starting to think he had made another bad decision.

The briefing room was packed on board the CCS Santa Cruz with Marine Corps officers and intelligence staff, as well as officers from other ships in the Fleet. Due to his recent experiences fighting the enemy shock troops he had been asked to attend, though from what he could see he was the lowest ranked person in the room. The ship was the sister of the vessel Spartan had served on board for many months but this was his new home. Unlike the other transports in the Fleet this one was dedicated to the transportation, support and supply of the elite commando companies. Every member of the commandos was selected from combat veterans with experience in the harshest of conditions. Spartan may have seen action in the bloodiest operation for the last fifty years but he had still only seen one action. Most of the marines sat there had a whole ten-year stint in the marines and a good half of them were back for another ten years.

General Rivers, an imposing figure dressed in his finest regalia, approached the front of the room. He was flanked by two marine guards, both in full armour and carrying L48 carbines in front of them on three point slings. Their armour covered them from head to toe and was completely sealed to allow them to move and fight in regions without atmosphere or pressure. Behind him marched Lieutenant Colonel Blake, leader of the commando company on board the ship and conspicuous by his camouflaged fatigues that he always wore. After the actions of the last weeks they were taking no chances with security and the armoured bodyguards were stationed all over the ship. He was an experienced warrior and had played an important part in the operations to remove the Zealot threat from the Titan Naval Station and transit stations in orbit around Proxima Prime.

"Please be seated," said General Rivers.

The room quietened as he stepped to the side and brought up a large display of the Proxima Centauri System, one of the three star systems in the Confederacy, the other two being Alpha Centauri and Sol, the old world that included the original capital of Earth. In the centre of the screen was the star, around it tracked the eleven planets of the system. Prime was the largest inhabited planet in the Proxima System and her naval station was the most significant outside of Alpha Centauri. The industrial planet of Kerberos was a close second in size to Prime and featured over a dozen inhabited moons and mining stations. The display focused in on Prime and stayed there as the General approached the microphone.

"This crisis has transformed from an insurgency on a small number of colonies to a general uprising that could threaten the very Confederacy. I have received word from Terra Nova that an assassination attempt on the President and key members of the Council was averted. We have only just heard, but due to the delay between Terra Nova and Proxima this took place two months ago. Since then we are receiving only sporadic transmissions, so for now we are on our own," he said seriously.

A hush spread through the hall at the news. The General lifted his hand for quiet. He continued.

"The good news is that there is no general support for the Zealots throughout the Confederacy. Their support base appears limited and if we act hard and fast we should be able to resolve this situation before it spirals. Our colonies are stable and the Fleet is under our control, but things can change and it is our job to protect the men and women of the Confederacy against any threat, from outside or within. Do not underestimate them though. They have been able to strike at ships in the Fleet and political figures on the ground. All Confed units have been activated and the reserves are being mobilised for a long campaign. Right now we need to stabilise the front lines, protect civilians and stop the attacks before the uprising spreads further. I will leave you in the hands of Lieutenant Colonel Blake who will explain the current tactical situation and outline your next operations. Good luck, I wish you well."

Lieutenant Colonel Blake took his place and saluted the General who marched off, still escorted by his personal guard.

"The operation to clear the satellites around Prime was a resounding success and the moon of Kronus and the Naval Station is under our control. Our losses were high but the objective was completed quickly and effectively. Starting today the engineering team is already clearing the damage on the Station and we expect it will be capable of receiving ships in less than a week."

Several of the marines cheered before spotting the stern look on the officer's face.

"That is the good part, I'm afraid the situation down on

Prime is much worse. We have important and very difficult work to do. As you are aware, most of the battlegroup that took part in ground operations on Kronus is undergoing resupply and medical attention. These forces are at the shipyard and medical station at Kerberos where they are expected to rejoin the battle if needed within two weeks. The last reinforcements from Alpha Centauri arrived two days ago and are already on the ground on Prime and are continuing the fight. The 3rd and 4th Marine Regiments have taken positions alongside those on Avagana. With the problem of communications with Terra Nova we can't expect any more help. As most of you know, the journey is forty-five weeks, so unless they are already on the way we are now without reinforcements. We have other problems, real problems," he said in a serious tone.

The officer zoomed in onto the continent where it showed the key mines, settlements, cities and transportation hubs. On the left side of the display was a large complex that was cantered around a huge city and surrounded by settlements, tower blocks and industrial sites. He zoomed out slightly so that the site of the Metallurgical Research & Mining Company showed along the side.

"Avagana, the Northern continent of Prime and home of its largest colony. As most of you are aware this is also the location of the Bone Mill."

He paused for a moment as those watching immediately recognised the most feared warzone in the System. In the last year a secretive religious group known as the Zealots had overrun the underground facility. Since then the Confederacy had been fighting to retake it. Several days before a force of genetically altered shock troopers had smashed out of the site and launched a lightning offensive against the marine and infantry units that encircled it. In hours hundreds of marines were dead and the enemy was advancing on the towns and settlements in the region. The name Bone Mill had come from the bitter underground combat between marine units and the insurgents. It signified the savage attrition that had seen few gains and hundreds of lives lost on both sides.

"You are all aware of the genetic threat the enemy pose since they unleashed what may only be described as their shock troops. We can only assume they have been developing this technology for some time, or that they have help from a third party, as until now their numbers have been small and their mode of operation discreet. These new shock troopers are something completely different and with them has arrived a new chapter in this struggle," he said as he waved over to Spartan.

Spartan felt a lump in his throat as he noticed everybody else in the room looking towards him. He had expected to be asked questions but the direct signal from the officer had still caught him by surprise.

"Private?" He beckoned to the front of the room where he was standing.

Spartan stood and made his way to the front, he could hear muttering and whispers from those present as he walked past. Although his combat experience on Kronus was undisputed, there was always jealously, and the fact that a mere private was being given the floor would do little to ingratiate him with them. He walked past the last row of officers and up to the Lieutenant Colonel. He stopped and saluted smartly.

"If you could provide us with your observations of the enemy," he said quietly.

The officer then took a step back so that Spartan stood alone. He moved to the mic and started to speak but his voice had gone completely dry. One of the marines stood nearby tilted his head, indicating for him to look to his right. He turned quickly and spotted the tray and the glasses of water, two sips and he felt much better. He cleared his throat and started again.

"Following the actions on Kronus, my team was tasked with boarding a small vessel escaping the scene of the battle. After boarding and securing the outer sections these creatures attacked us. They definitely look human, though I'm not sure how or what has changed them. Their muscles are thicker and the jaws and bones have expanded and strengthened. The ones we faced were able to break through armour and also absorb heavy trauma from our weapons' fire."

Spartan turned back and took another sip of water.

Before he could continue, two of the officers in the room stood up.

"Yes?" Spartan asked.

"Captain MacArthur, Bravo Company. From your encounter would you not describe them as animals, or are you saying they are a modified or mutated form of human?"

"I couldn't say where they are from, it is clear that they are capable of using weapons and working as a group. I didn't hear them speak or communicate, but I was kind of busy," he said with a grin.

A gentle laughter ran about through the hall and Spartan finally started to relax. The Captain sat down but the second officer was still standing. Spartan couldn't quite make him out but he wore the fatigues of one of the combat units.

"Are these the same creatures as the ones that broke out of the Bone Mill?" he asked.

"From what I have seen I can confirm that these are the same creatures that we saw on Prime."

Spartan turned to the officers behind him and then stepped away from the microphone. The Lieutenant Colonel approached him and spoke quietly.

"Thank you, Private, you may return." He then continued to speak from the podium. Spartan went back to his seat.

"As you can see, these troops are tougher than anything

you have faced before. They are hard to kill and have the strength and ferocity to match. How they are controlled or where their loyalties lie is unknown to us, just as their origins are. What we do know is that while the uprising consists of just tens of thousands of people, the number of these new shock troopers is much more. The initial waves were more than twenty thousand and more still keep emerging from under the ground. What we can't tell is whether they are modified human subjects or if they have been built from scratch. They are capable of using a variety of tools and weapons, including edged weapons and firearms. From the specimens brought back by our forces it seems these things may be human in some way and that they have been engineered to do a specific job. That job is war and they are damned, damned good at it!" he said loudly.

On the screen a profile of one of the creatures appeared, it showed the reinforced armour, tougher muscles and also several video sequences of them in close combat. They moved fast and were capable of biting or ripping people apart without the use of weapons. One image also showed a creature wearing armour and carrying a projectile weapon on its shoulder. Another showed a group of people, some of them wearing the robes of the Zealots but many more looked like civilians, though all were armed in some way.

"The combat situation is grave. Our forces in Avagana have been hit on multiple fronts and always from the underground facilities controlled by the Zealots. We are seeing a mixture of enemy units and not all the civilians appear to be Zealots. Whether this means their support base is spreading or that these are a less extreme version of the group we cannot tell. What we do know is that after the initial attack all military units have been forced on the defensive. Our forces have been trying to hold back the assaults to keep the towns and cities clear. I can tell you all that this operation to halt their advance has failed. The enemy continue to emerge from the Bone Mill and the many mines and tunnels that it is connected to over an area of three hundred square kilometres. We can only assume they have the ability to construct these soldiers at a fast rate. Alternatively, they may have been holding them in hiding all this time and are moving them through the many uncharted caves, tunnels and manmade shafts that exist down there."

The image changed to show a much closer view of the planet.

"We have launched three raids into the underground sites to obtain intelligence. Every single one of these has failed and more of these creatures keep emerging. We have therefore been authorised to conduct a series of air strikes to neutralise the entire complex before their numbers become unmanageable. This however will only stop the reinforcements of the enemy, those in the field must still be dealt with," he explained.

The display zoomed in to a snaking river along which straddled a massive city and port.

"This is New Carlos, capital of the colony and home to over thirty million people. It is one of the newest mega cities in the Confederacy and the largest city on Prime. The Governor is missing and presumed dead following a series of suicide bombings. We have already started to evacuate the smaller towns and mining outposts but we don't have enough aircraft to complete the evacuation. The order has already been issued that all citizens should move to their nearest city. There are nine major cities in the colony and all have been hit to varying degrees."

The map zoomed out and each city was highlighted in red to show the dispersal of the population. The continent was substantial, almost the size of North America on Earth. After pausing on the wider view for a few seconds, the map rolled out into a flat two-dimensional display showing the entire planet's surface. Thick green lines split the planet up into the Seven Colonies of Prime.

"Our military garrisons in the colonies are already mobilising army units to help with the fighting but it will take hours, in some cases days, for them to reach Avagana. There is also the problem of escalation, if the troubles spread to the other colonies on Prime the military forces could be easily pinned down." He moved the map to zoom in to the mega city.

"New Carlos cannot fall. Apart from the population

of the colony at present in and around the city, it is also connected directly to the Carlos Spaceport. It is the largest transport hub in this part of the Avagana Colony and the most important one on the planet. There are road, rail and water links from this point that lead to the other colonies on Prime. It is one of the few sites that can handle the heavy transports and landers in the Fleet. If the enemy takes New Carlos they will control the pivotal section of the planet. Even of more concern, they will wipe out or assimilate every citizen in the area. In the last forty-eight hours Confed forces have been assisting the civilians in a general evacuation of the regions around the Bone Mill and the remote towns along the coast of Avagana. They are directing them to the cities. There is a problem though."

The map zoomed to a section below the city showing icons where the various units were situated. A line of black ran in a broken line along with multiple red blocks moving towards the area.

"Three of the towns west of this point have been overrun and their citizens are running for New Carlos. Elements of the 7th Marine Regiment are trying to hold back the enemy as the civilians fall back to the city. So far they are holding but our best estimates are that they will last for only two, maybe three hours. With that back door open the enemy will stream into the undefended sections of the city. I think you can image what happens from there," he said solemnly.

The room was now completely silent as the marines started to understand he gravity of the situation. The creatures that had been unleashed on the population by the Zealots were smashing their way through the Confed cordons and heading for all the populated zones. It was all going far worse than any of them had expected. He continued.

"Reports from the overrun town of Carnaz indicate that the Zealots are not wiping out population centres. When the shock troops took the town they killed anyone who opposed them but left the civilian population. Their new shock troops have been in the field now for four days and show no signs of stopping. When the troops moved on they left the area for the Zealots to secure. Once they arrived they started to sort through those that were left. Troublemakers are being sent to camps for whatever nefarious plans they might have, the rest are staying in their homes. This is consistent with our understanding of their plans. It would appear they wish to replace the leadership of Prime, not the population. This leads our intelligence units to conclude that there may be a more significant threat than just the Zealots behind the attacks. It appears there is a large political element behind the uprising."

On the screen the display shifted to show multiple military units and their commanders' profiles. One man stood out amongst them all, a sixty-four year old army general.

"General Shears, Commander of all planetary forces on Prime has taken command of New Carlos and is mustering a mixed force of army, marines and city militia to help defend the city. He has already mobilised over twelve thousand fighters but he needs more time. They have only been able to fortify twenty percent of the perimeter and the enemy has now reached the outskirts of the city. We have conducted air operations against them but they are too close for us to risk bombardments that near to civilians. They are moving fast on the defences but not fast enough to do the job, that is where you come in!"

"The Santa Cruz and our commandos are to spearhead a dangerous operation to blunt the enemy assault to give General Shears enough time to finish the basic defences for the city. At the same time three army transports have just arrived from Alpha Centauri. They will follow us in and provide reinforcements for General Shears in the upcoming siege. This will be a hit and run operation, we do not have the numbers to hold them indefinitely. Just get in there fast, cause as much mess as you can and then get out. I have a list of missions for you all to carry out but for now this is the priority. Briefings have been sent to your computer units. Have your squads ready for drops in sixty minutes!"

As he walked off Spartan looked around the room, noting the number of marines running in different directions. Since his transfer to the ship he hadn't actually taken part in a combat mission. He moved from his chair and headed for the door before being cut off by the approaching officers. One of them, a tall man with a rough face and a smile stopped in front of him.

"Sergeant Spartan," said Captain Mathews. He looked at the marine noticing his rank was back to private.

"Sir," said Spartan as he saluted.

The Captain was in charge of Alpha Company and they had met during the action to retake the Naval Station. He had been instrumental in getting Spartan promoted to start with.

"I see your rank didn't stick. Well, don't worry about it, there's plenty of work to do and work in the Marine Corps usually means quick promotion. That was a damned good job back on Kronus. As you might expect though, it's not going to get any easier."

"Understood, Sir."

"How is Teresa? Her injuries?" He looked genuinely concerned.

"She's doing well, the doctors say she will be fit for duty in a four to five days."

"Fast, very fast. I'm impressed, she'll be an asset to the unit."

"Yeah," said Spartan as he thought about his closest friend in the Fleet.

They were close, very close but the constant training

and action over the last days had made it difficult to spend any real time together. He hoped a lull in the fighting would give them a chance to take some leave, but when that might happen he had no idea. They started to make slow progress towards the door before the Captain stopped.

"How is the new unit going? I know you've been thrown in the deep end but we need the quickest and strongest for the commandos. We have a habit of getting through people pretty fast!" he laughed.

"They're not the easiest people to get on with, Sir. I'm not complaining, it's just the way it us with a new unit. A combat operation will clear things up I'm sure," he answered wryly.

"Indeed. Now, I understand you've already worked with Lieutenant Daniels?"

Spartan inhaled, his facial expressions did him a disservice as he tried to look as impassive as he could. The officer certainly wasn't the worst Spartan had met, but he lacked experience and at their last encounter he had felt a certain amount of rivalry that shouldn't exist between a ranker like him and an officer.

"Yes, Sir, he led one of the units in the final assault on the Naval Station."

"I know he's a little green but his training and combat record is exemplary. He has been assigned temporary command of one of the engineering platoons. Based upon your experience with the armour, and with him, I would like you to take a position in his platoon as second sergeant. The rest of your squad has been assigned to him and is already going over the briefing."

"I assumed my promotion was just a temporary rank, Sir? I've only just finished basic training and I thought the move to the Cruz was to be part of my training as a commando. I was told when I arrived on the ship I was to be returned to private in my new unit."

"You've already completed most of the commando training and your combat experience and the operations over the next weeks will either make or break you as a commando," he said.

Spartan's current status was confused as he had only just been promoted. The battle to take the Station had been Spartan's first military operation, and though it lasted just hours he had probably been involved in more action than most marines would face in an entire career. Even so, when he had landed he was no more than a private. Due to the heavy losses in the assault he had been given a battlefield promotion to sergeant. He had acquitted himself well enough for an immediate transfer to the commando unit aboard the Marine Transport ship CCS Santa Cruz. Captain Mathews continued.

"Daniels' unit is the newest one here. Most of the NCOs are either on the way here or were injured in the fighting on Kronus. There is nobody else with the kind of experience the unit needs. You have the position for now if you want it."

"For now?" asked Spartan.

"Well, once we're fully reinforced there will only be so many positions available. Traditionally the post is based partially on service time and partially on merit. You'll have to compete with the old timers. My suggestion is just keep doing what you do well and I'm sure the job will be yours. Think of this as an opportunity to make your rank more... permanent," he said with a look that told Spartan exactly what he needed to hear.

The Captain stepped in a little closer as if he had something important he needed to say but didn't want to be overheard.

"A number of the officers have mentioned your tactical use of the engineers in combat and we have already been authorised to assign Daniels use of the full company's worth of equipment for this operation. It will give him enough equipment for a full platoon. We've only used the gear for sappers' work so far but you have already proved the combat effectiveness of the armour and strength, both on the ground and in zero-g environments. I think the Lieutenant would appreciate your support in their use on the drop. The techs on board have already started to modify some of the armour based on your exploits. Apparently, Spartan, you retrofitted weapons during one of the training exercises?"

"Well, I'm not sure that using gaffer tape to strap

training weapons to engineering gears really qualified as retrofitting, Sir."

"Really? You have a lot to learn then!" the Captain laughed.

The two men continued towards the side of the hall, only a few marines remained, some were making notes or discussing the upcoming operation with their officers.

"Did you say an entire platoon, Sir?" asked a surprised Spartan, still unsure as to what was going on.

"Yes, I've recommended the entire platoon will be armoured for this operation. Take it from me, with the numbers you'll be facing you'll want the armour and the weapons! This isn't a permanent unit, we just need as much fighting power on the surface as we can get."

A marine approached them and waited patiently for the Captain to turn to him. He handed over a datapad and the Captain gave it just the quickest of glances.

"Sergeant, I must go. Get to Daniels in Section 3F and do whatever you need to get this mission done. Remember the briefing, New Carlos must not fall! Good luck on the mission, let me know how the armour works out!"

Without waiting for a reply the Captain marched off and out of the briefing room. Spartan stood on his own looking around. He'd only just joined his new unit and this new promotion wasn't going to win him any friends. He lifted his datapad and checked for the location of Section 3F where the unit was preparing for action. It wasn't far away, just three sections down the ship and after the armoury. He left the room and entered the side shaft that ran the length of the ship. There were no windows on this part and it was just as well, as the movement of the stars when viewed from the rotating section of the vessel were known to cause nausea and sickness. As he marched down the shaft he noticed the large number of marine commandos equipping for combat. These units were normally based on the Furious Battlegroup but most of the ships were still being prepared for the conflict and the battalion had been rushed to the frontline on numerous transports and craft. The downside was that a large part of the heavy equipment was still back at the naval base on Kerberos. For now the CCS Santa Cruz was the new home for the 5thReconnaissance Battalion of the Confederate Marine Corps. Though it lacked space for the heavy armour and weapons of the unit it did have a number of landing craft and shuttles on board, as well as the engineering equipment and armour that Spartan would be making use of.

The entire unit usually made use of light armoured vehicles and gunships to deliver small teams into combat. The 5th was an elite battalion of the Marine Corps and consisted of over a thousand men and women, the best the Marine Corps had to offer. It was made up of a Headquarters and Services Company, three commando companies and finally the elite Force Reconnaissance

Company. The battalion provided reconnaissance and surveillance for the rest of the Corps. They were also trained in close quarters battle (CQB) tactics and other special missions. They were expected to be able to carry out any operation with speed and efficiency. There was no mission they couldn't complete, or at least that is what they said repeatedly to themselves.

Spartan walked past two women who were in the process of fitting on their Personal Defence Suits. These were the standard set of clothing, camouflage and tactical armour used by all CMC Marines. It was lightweight and covered the entire surface of the marine. As he moved away from them and to the automatic door that led to the next section his mind shifted to Teresa. They met when first joining as recruits and they had become much more than just close friends. In the combat landing on the Naval Station she had taken serious wounds. The ground fire had been much stronger than expected and many marines had been killed trying to establish a beachhead. She was recovering fast and he really wanted to see her but time wasn't on his side. He would have to check in on her on his return.

The door slid shut behind him and he continued on to the final section where his platoon was assembling. The entrance to the hangars and loading bays was much more utilitarian in appearance than the rest of the ship. Weapon lockers and stowage containers were everywhere. Along the left side of the corridor were dozens of mechanical suits designed for use in repairing and maintaining the ship, or for use on combat operations with the engineers company. These military suits were similar to the sealed Personal Defence Suits but much thicker and bulkier. Known as the Combat Engineer Suits or CES they were of much sturdier construction and also equipped with heavy-duty hydraulic gear, digging implements and cutting tools. Some of the suits were fitted with close range weapons but, since Spartan's training and combat experience, in the last few days the equipment was already being heavily modified. As he walked past the fifth suit he noticed something odd about it. He stopped and looked carefully, trying to work out way it was so familiar.

"You okay, Marine?" asked one of the fitters.

Spartan looked at the man and then again at the suit. "Yeah, this one looks familiar."

"Well, it should do, it's one of the suits used for the boarding action a few days back. I've patched some of the holes and welded in the plating as recommended by the report put together by Private Morato."

"Teresa recommended this? Strange, she never mentioned it."

"Yeah, the reports we were given from the survivors of the Titan mission said the suits were vulnerable to hits on some of the hydraulic sections and also there's thinner plating near the ribs. We've not had time to fit in all the recommendations but we have sealed the biggest weaknesses and fitted the weapons as per the comments in the report," explained the man as he continued making adjustments.

Spartan continued on towards the group of marines at the end of the room. There were two platoons getting ready. The first was from Charlie Company and were readying their weapons and armour. Each marine wore a PDS suit and carried the marine's standard issue L48 12.7mm assault rifle. The weapon used a twenty round magazine of variable operation ammunition and it was equally suited for short and long-range work. It had proven itself against a variety of enemies and types of armour. One marine in each squad carried the 6mm module and box magazine that modified the standard L48 rifle into a support weapon that could unleash massive quantities of lower calibre ammunition. It was normally used on board ships where hull penetration could be an issue.

Several of the marines acknowledged him as he walked past the first group and up to where his own platoon was assembling. The unit was made up of three squads and led by Lieutenant Daniels. He was busy discussing some piece of equipment with the crew Chief. Spartan stopped and saluted.

"Sergeant Spartan, glad to see you're finally here. I thought we'd lost you."

"I've just finished speaking with Captain Mathews, he

requested I join your unit, Sir."

"Yes...he did," answered Daniels.

The officer turned away and finished his discussion with the Chief before turning back to Spartan.

"Contrary to what you might think, I am glad to have you here, Spartan," he said as he handed over a datapad. "As you can see, we are to be dropped into the most violent and dangerous part of the battle on the surface."

Spartan examined the maps and dispositions in detail. The datapad viewed the events in real-time and the scale of the battle was enormous. The main part appeared to be about five hundred metres from the city limits where a collapsed tunnel forced the focal point of the enemy assault. Scores of marines and infantry were battling in the rubble but, even as Spartan watched, the enemy shock troopers were smashing their way through the thin lines of defenders.

"How are the defences along the city limits coming along?" he asked.

"We are working fast, but if they break through the outer marker they will be inside the city in minutes. We need to clear an area of two hundred and fifty metres wide for an hour so heavy weapons and minefields can be set up. General Shears is sending five companies of city militia to help but they will not be able to hold the line until the defences are finished."

One of the crew ran up to them and spoke directly to

Spartan. The man was short and covered in grease and oil from working on the machines.

"Your suit is ready, Sergeant."

Spartan nodded and turned back to the Lieutenant. "How long till we start the drop?"

Daniels checked his watch before replying. "We will be over the drop point in eleven minutes, we start the drop immediately, you'd better get ready."

"Will do, good luck, Sir," Spartan said as he delivered a crisp salute.

As Daniels moved off to get himself ready the first three CES units stomped past. Each was much bigger than a man and looked like an armoured monster. They were all painted in grey but a few carried the personal markings and patterns of the squad and unit commanders. Spartan approached his own unit and pushed his legs inside. Two of the crew helped to fit him in as they clamped down the seals and plates around his body. It wasn't a vehicle, more a heavy and augmented suit that was perfectly suited to hostile environments. As the metal rings around the neck locked into place he felt the air pressure change as the suit fully sealed. Through the metal reinforced visor he could see the crew hammering with tools as the last sections were clamped into place. One woman stopped in front of him and peered inside his helmet.

"Sergeant Spartan, your suit has been modified as per the specifications in Private Morato's paper. The welding and repair tools have been removed. We have retained one utility blade on the left arm mount and the right is fitted with twin L48 carbines. Both are loaded with 6mm box magazines and are linked through to the digging controls on the right panel."

Spartan looked about inside the suit and found the small bank of recently added switches. The job wasn't pretty but for just a few days' work it was impressive.

"Good work, I'll let you know how it all works out!"

The woman banged her wrench on the helmet as a signal it was clear to move. Two more CES units marched past and Spartan moved in behind them as they filed ahead. Walking along the left side of the column of armoured marines were the men and woman of Charlie Company. In comparison their PDS suits looked puny and weak.

The massive airlock door was open. It led to the loading bay for the landing craft. Each craft was heavily armoured and designed to carry a full platoon of over forty marines. In this particular action the CES units took up twice the space of a marine. Three of the mighty machines were waiting with their side ramps down for their passengers to board. The marines filed in, the CES units first and the rest of the marines squeezing in around them. Spartan approached the third craft and found he was the second CES unit to board the vessel. As he attached the clamps to his suit one of the marines spotted him.

"Hey, Sergeant, thought you'd abandoned us!" shouted

Harrison.

He was one of the few marines he'd met in the last few days since arriving on the ship. He was a jovial character and one hell of a card player. Wherever Harrison was, Anthony always seemed to be there as well. Spartan looked around and sure enough he could see the other man. Then he saw two people he thought he'd managed to avoid for months. Burnett and Matt, two of the recruits from when he first joined.

"Spartan?" The first one asked.

He just looked at them. "Sergeant Spartan," he answered.

Burnett approached and looked through his helmet. "What's your first name, dude?"

"Sergeant," he answered as he unclipped his right armoured hand swinging it around in front of the two marines.

"What are you doing here?" A third man approached, he was tall and wearing a fire-scorched suit. It was a mark of pride to repair the damage but not to remove the marks on the exterior of armour. This man had seen some trouble. Spartan recognised him and relaxed.

"It's me, Marcus. A few of us were shipped over earlier today to fill out some of the units in the 5th. I take it you've already met these two?" he laughed.

The two marines had already moved away and were talking to each other quietly. They'd found themselves in a fight with Spartan on the very first day and he had no doubt they were still looking for some kind of payback from the bloody nose he gave them. Marcus on the other hand was a different person altogether. They'd fought together on the Station and Marcus was injured during the assault.

"What about the leg, I thought you'd been hit?"

"Yeah, still hurts. Took a 9mm round in the calf. They patched me up though, managed to avoid any serious damage. Somebody up there still likes me!"

The lights in the craft began flashing and the doors started to close shut.

"Secure all gear and personnel, combat drop in sixty seconds," came the voice over the speakers.

With a loud clunk the doors shut and sealed. Almost as soon as they had shut the outer doors on the hull of the ship slid open to reveal the planet below. Spartan looked through the small slits running along the side of the craft to see the planet moving. The section the landing craft was on still rotated around the exterior of the ship. As he watched the planet appeared above and arced downwards. It was odd but the system was simple. The clamps would be released, the outwards force on the rotating section would cast the craft out into space, much like a person letting go on a merry go round though at much slower speeds.

"5, 4, 3, 2...1," came a computerised voice.

With a shudder the craft released from the ship and pushed off towards Prime. From gaps running along the sides of his craft Spartan watched the other two landing craft launch and move into position along side them. Over twenty more were assembling in the little flotilla that would carry three full companies of commandos and CES units into action. A slight kick indicated the engines firing up and the craft accelerated into orbit and on its long arcing path through the atmosphere.

CHAPTER TWO

The development of capital ships started after the end of the Great War after one of the outer colonies in the Alpha Centauri had done the unthinkable and split from the Confederacy. For a time it looked like others would follow the example of Carthago and another war would split apart the fragile alliance. With eight rebel warships under their command they looked impregnable.

It took an emergency flotilla to be assembled from every vessel still operational in the Alpha Centauri System and a violent battle that lasted three days before Carthago yielded. Since that fateful year the Confederate Navy has ensured it always controls larger, faster and more powerful vessels than those of the individual colonies.

Origins of the Battlecruiser

The CCS Crusader, the newest and deadliest ship in the Confederation military had just reached the outer markers around Kerberos, one of the eleven planets in the Proxima Centauri Star System. She was the flagship of the Confederate Navy and on her way home from the epic Siege of Titan after sustaining heavy damage and massive casualties. The battle had been unlike anything in the last fifty years and the repairs to the ship would probably takes months of hard work. The vessel moved into orbit around Kerberos as it steamed dust and debris from the dozens of damaged sections.

From space the planet of Kerberos gave off an odd greenish blue glow. Many people in the Confederacy considered the planet to be the most Earth-like of all the worlds but it was actually very different. The gravity and atmosphere were comparable but the air was much thinner. This made it difficult for the elderly or people with respiratory problems. This was one of the many reasons why the limited surface area had been built on so fast, creating insulated buildings with improved air supplies. Since it had been colonised the single super continent had been built up with thousands of tall buildings, a testament to the massive factories and workshops dotting the landscape.

Kerberos was an industrial world and although the factories and shipyards in Alpha Centauri were more famous for their quality and size, the new worlds in Proxima had proven cheap and competitive. The exports from the new colonies on Kerberos and Prime were almost reaching the same quantities of the old worlds.

This growing competition increased the demands on the neighbouring planets and moons for raw materials. The massive increase in manufacturing had its problems though. The increase in mining and transport had created more than a few accidents. Even more of a problem was the never-ending scourge of pirates and organised crime. The riskier the businesses the more unsavoury the people involved were. Though Kerberos wasn't the most populated of the planets it was where much of the technology and heavy equipment in the Proxima System was manufactured. Massive shipyards in orbit built transports and passenger liners that ploughed their way through the busy shipping lanes. One of the largest shipyards contained the half completed hulk of the sister battlecruiser to Crusader. This new vessel had already been lengthened by ten percent. This was to accommodate a set of hangars to carry either a number of gunboats or transports for marine detachments. A frigate was moored a short distance away keeping a watchful eye over the building project.

The main shipping lanes had already been cleared to allow the remnants of the Fleet to move into position around the orbital shipyards. Normally the vessels would have stayed at the Titan Naval Station at Prime but the Station had been badly damaged during the battle and subsequent sabotage. It was quicker to limp to Kerberos than wait for the docks and yards to be repaired sufficiently to allow work on the warships. What normally would take a matter of seven or eight hours had taken the ship three days. The Crusader was massive, though in space its size was only apparent when she approached other vessels. The hull looked as if it was wrapped in a series of bands rotating in unison around the structure of the ship. These bands along the hull provided full and half gravity to the vessel and its crew. She normally travelled with a full complement of over two thousand personnel and two hundred heavily equipped marines. Following the battle with the captured battleship CCS Victorious, the Crusader had sustained very heavy damage and the casualties amongst the crew were terrible. One of the reactors was still leaking and over half of her weapon systems were burnt out or destroyed.

Commander Anderson, the ship's Executive Officer, was in command and his face showed sheer exhaustion from the last few days' events. He was a man of slender build, with a freckled face and light brown unkempt hair. Like many of the naval officers he wore smartly trimmed sideburns and a small moustache. His uniform hadn't been changed since the battle and it was crumpled and grubby. A dark bloodstain had smudged along the chest though it wasn't clear whose blood it was. He was an experienced officer and had previously served with the Navy Cutter squadrons out in the wilderness on the Rim. It was an area of space that divided the colonised planets of Proxima and the outer gas giants. Much like the asteroid belt in the old Solar System it was packed with millions of tumbling rocks and asteroids, some the size of small planets and moons.

The Rim was the heart of the mining and refining operations for many private corporations. With its many hiding places it had also become a haven for pirates and organised crime. There had once been a naval station there but it was destroyed in the Great War and never rebuilt. Commander Anderson had earned his reputation in a year-long campaign where he had led a wing of six cutters in the region. Operating from a modified frigate the group had captured over thirty known criminals as well as shutting down two of their bases. It had earned him the reputation as an aggressive but highly successful leader. He was a rising star in the Fleet. Becoming the executive officer on the CCS Crusader, the flagship of the entire Confederation Fleet, had been a great honour and the high point of his career. One day he hoped to command a vessel like the Crusader into battle at the head of a fleet. But for now he was babysitting the warhorse as she made her slow progress to the yards.

In the last few days the tense and critical role of

helping to manage such a massive vessel had turned into something much more exciting. Instead of managing crew rosters and weapon systems, he had been thrown into something much more violent than anything he had experienced so far. As well as assisting in the running of the tactical operations during the Siege of Titan, he had also been on the bridge during the epic battle with the rebel battleship CCS Victorious. The battle had lasted a long time and hundreds and hundreds of crew had been lost in the desperate broadsides and boarding actions. Though Crusader had emerged the victor the ship had sustained 427 dead and 719 wounded. Only 42 of the entire 200 man marine force on board had survived boarding actions and violent broadsides of the battle between the two massive capital ships. This meant the warship had lost over half of her crew, though many of the injured were still manning their posts as she limped home. The ship was now more a slow moving memorial to the dead and injured than a deadly warship capable of facing any known vessel.

Until two days ago, Admiral Jarvis had still been aboard helping to organise the evacuation of the damaged and crippled warships. The Admiral had not been happy at sending the heavily damaged ship away, but with leaks in the reactor there was a chance the ship would lose power and end up dead in space. More ships were on their way from the rest of the Confederacy but it would be days before anything the size of the heavy cruiser or a battleship would arrive. Vessels of this size could conduct all kinds of missions from orbital bombardments to blockade management as well as the job they were mainly built for, combat against other vessels.

With space operations now focused on the blockade of Prime and the transport of personnel to the surface she had since transferred her flag to the escort carrier CCS Wasp. This vessel was almost as large as the Crusader but it was optimised as an escort carrier. As well as being able to handle the heavy gunboats used to escort shuttles and landing craft, it was also designed to operate as a command ship for amphibious operations. From there the Admiral could work alongside General Rivers in coordinating the action on and around Prime.

Hovering around the battered ship like a swarm of angry flies were gunboats of the Kerberos Squadron. This unit had already sent most of its warships to assist in operations at Prime. A number of the smaller vessels had remained, as well as the scores of gunboats that helped protect the infrastructure and ships orbiting the planet. The gunboats were tiny when compared to the warship but their size was deceptive. Each craft contained masses of weapons and electronic jamming equipment. In sufficient numbers they could take on small warships like cutters and frigates. Against civilian craft just one or two was enough to force a course change or demand inspections.

On board the Crusader lights started to flash on the

communication panel. Lieutenant Nilsson, a dark brown haired officer with distinctive, green tinted brown eyes, examined the data coming from her communication desk. At first she thought it was one of the many malfunctions stemming from the damage they had sustained in battle. It quickly became clear that the indications were pointing to a narrow band burst transmission from the planet's surface. She turned to the Executive Officer.

"Sir, I'm picking up encoded traffic on narrow band from the planet below."

The Commander walked towards her desk and examined the data himself. His face contorted in confusion.

"I don't understand. Narrow band is focused at a specific point. How are we picking it up unless it is meant for us?"

"It must be, Sir, unless it's an accident."

"I don't think so. There's a lot of space out here and the odds are miniscule. If it weren't for us then who would it be for in this orbit? Can you decode it?"

I'm working on it, Sir, just give me a moment…" she replied, as she worked fervently on the system.

A series of coloured bars flashed on the display until a group of visual locks were removed to reveal a final security layer. Lieutenant Nilsson sighed before turning back to him.

"The message is encoded in a book-based cipher, only part of it makes sense without the code book, I have forwarded it to your datapad."

Commander Anderson picked his pad up and entered his security code to gain access. He was surprised to find just a few lines of information from a source he didn't recognise. There were details of several civilian ships and something or somebody called 'The One' and a list of nine buildings on the planet below. He recognised one of them as the Presidential Complex. Beneath the lists were two lines, both in some form of a cipher and one he had not seen before. At the top of the message was a coded word, presumably the name of the subject or certainly an identifying code. He didn't recognise any of the words but the first line would be a good start. He was about to hand the material back for analysis when he noticed a prefix code used on board the Confederation ships and depots for access to low security areas. It was changed daily and this code had only been initiated in the last four hours.

"Gods!" he swore to himself.

He fumbled as he highlighted the code at the start of the document and transferred it back to Lieutenant Nilsson.

"The message has been encoded with an unknown cipher. This could be a serious breach. I need you to find out who it was intended for as quickly as possible!"

She looked at the text and started feeding it into various analysis tools but the data didn't match any of the known Naval coding systems. She started the polymorphic analysis engine normally used to assess and monitor electronic jamming and sensory data. The computer system was the most advanced in the Fleet and could handle multiple wide band data streams and decode them in real-time. At first the system appeared stuck then it started to pick up key parts of the cipher.

"Commander, it shouldn't be more than a few minutes."

A light on the ship-to-ship communication channel started to flicker and she tapped the voice communications unit to activate audio. The authorisation signature of the Admiral popped up on her terminal. She turned around and caught the attention of Commander Anderson.

"Sir, incoming transmission from Admiral Jarvis."

The Commander signalled for her to put the message through.

"Admiral," he said as her image appeared on the screen.

"Commander, I take it you're taking good care of my ship?" she asked with barely a smile.

"Of course," he replied.

"I have just received word from General Shears on the surface of Prime that the colony of New Georgia is siding against us."

"Against us? I don't understand, Admiral."

"It would appear that the sentiment of the general public, or at least their politicians, is that Confed Forces have no business on Colony territory. I suspect some of them must be colluding with the Zealots."

"That could explain how they have been hiding so

many troops underground for so long," he said scratching his chin.

"Perhaps. Either way it looks like the troubles on the surface are about to become a whole lot more complicated. The official line from New Georgia is that they have declared the presence of Confederation Infantry as an occupying force on their territory. They have given all military units on Prime a twelve-hour ultimatum to leave or be interned. The other five colonies are in an emergency session of the Council of Seven, I don't know how it is going to pan out, but knowing how this is starting to unravel I think we could be facing ground war."

"What can I do, Admiral?"

"I need this to go private."

Commander Anderson lifted a headset from the computer terminal and flicked a switch that closed off the audio from the main speaker system.

"We're secure."

"Good. I have an intelligence team on Kerberos that I am waiting to hear from. They are investigating a potential terrorist cell with intel on the insurgency. I am expecting to receive important information in the twenty-four hours…" she said before the Commander interrupted her.

"What are you expecting them to find?"

"There have been rumours for some time in certain circles that something is going on between the mega corporations on Kerberos and the left-wing religious faction and their militant off-shoots."

"Interesting. We have already received an encoded narrowband transmission from the surface, we are in the process of accessing the data now," he said.

" I doubt that will be my contact on Kerberos, he's not due to commence his operation for at least another hour. Who else knows about the signal?" she asked quickly.

"Just myself and Lieutenant Nilsson."

There was an audible sigh from the Admiral before she continued.

"Good, make sure it stays that way. The situation here is very delicate, as is the intelligence operation on Kerberos. When you have the data contact me, I need to know how far this goes and what contacts the groups on Kerberos have made. Good luck, Commander, we will speak soon."

"Understood, Admiral," he said as he replaced the headset and turned back to the Lieutenant.

* * *

The ride through the lower atmosphere of Prime was rough and Spartan was forced to grip the thick metal handrails, as the clamps holding up his suit didn't seem to be doing the job. One of the other CES suits had already broken loose and crushed the arm of one of the marines waiting patiently for the landing to commence. His shouting had echoed through the pressurised interior of the landing craft. It did little to help ease the tension that always preceded an operation like this one. Unlike travelling through space, the friction of the lower atmosphere was thick and created massive amounts of heat along the body of their landing craft. These parts of the flight were always dangerous, as any weakness in the skins of the craft could let in the heat and destroy the craft in an instant. That, plus the knowledge of the battle waiting ahead, was the ultimate sobering thought for Spartan. A final shudder came from the craft as it settled into a lower speed and more conformable flight.

Though Spartan had been in the Marine Corps for less than a year he had seen two combat drops already. One had been a contested landing on the moon of Kronus, the home of the now infamous Titan Naval Station. His second operation had been a much smaller one, though ultimately more dangerous action in space. He, along with a small unit of marines, had boarded a craft escaping from the burning hulk of CCS Victorious. On both occasions he had seen many good marines die and that had been just a few days earlier. He had expected to find some action in the Corps but nothing had led him to believe he would be facing three operations in less than five days!

"I'm gonna need a damned vacation!" he muttered to himself.

A crackle followed by a high-pitched whine indicated an impending announcement. That or the equipment had just malfunctioned.

"Marines, we hit the ground in four minutes. Hold on, we're going in hot," came the voice of the pilot.

On the wall behind the cockpit was a video display with maps and communication feeds to the units already in action. It had been switched off during the rough trip through the atmosphere, as the signal was unusable during re-entry.

"Man, can you see that shit?" Marcus was examining the moving map.

Spartan looked closely. It showed the outer perimeter and about a hundred people fighting in a series of ruined buildings. Blasts from charges and grenades flickered along the line but the greater numbers of shock troops were starting to break through. At two points in the line breaches had been made.

"They aren't going to last long against that," said Spartan.

The screen flashed and was replaced with the face of Lieutenant Daniels, the leader of the platoon. He was sat up front with the pilots in the most heavily armoured section of the craft.

"Marines, you're about to land in the most violent warzone I have seen in my military career. I have also received word of trouble spreading through the other colonies on Prime. New Carlos is the largest city on the planet and the most important inhabited region in this entire System. It is imperative that you clear the outer markers so the engineer teams can establish a firm perimeter. This is a tough assignment. That is why we've been chosen. Stand strong and listen to your platoon commanders. Watch your comrades and remember your training. Good luck!"

The message flickered and then cut back to the map.

"Another message from our fearless leader!" said one of the marines as he banged his rifle magazine on his head.

"Sixty seconds!" the pilot shouted.

A hiss spread through the craft as the vessel depressurised. Although the marines were all wearing fully enclosed suits, the craft were always pressurised to provide full protection for the crew and passengers in case of any equipment or armour faults during space operations. It was also common for the craft to carry unarmoured passengers, especially when used for medical evacuation or transport missions. The system was fast and in just seconds the indicator on Spartan's suit confirmed the status of the vessel. The metal shutters clunked open a few centimetres, giving each of the marines their first view of the warzone. As the shutters moved into position the escape hatches and access ramps disarmed, ready for landing under fire. The last thing the marines needed was to be trapped on board stuck in a firefight.

On both sides of the craft were great clouds of black smoke from the many fires spread around the countryside and outskirts of the city. On the sides of the landing craft were door guns, each one a large calibre projectile weapon capable of shredding a man. They were used to fend off light aircraft or to provide ground support during a landing. Spartan had used one in the low gravity ground conflict on the Naval Station and had experienced the devastating firepower of the weapons firsthand. With their speed reducing, the gunners moved to their exposed positions along the sides of the craft. The weapons unlocked from their secure, armoured lockers where they were kept safe during re-entry.

Jackson looked up to Spartan who was busy checking the settings in his suit.

"You ready, man?"

"Hell, yeah!" he said with a grimace.

"Is Daniels coming down with us or is he staying with the ship?" Marcus asked.

As if to answer the question the figure of the Lieutenant appeared. He wasn't wearing any armour and for a moment Spartan and Marcus were confused. Then the Lieutenant turned and pulled himself inside his CES armour. Two of the marines helped seal him in.

"Hell, do you think he could have left it a bit later?"

"Maybe he was hoping to stay with the boat, Marcus?" said one of the marines who had been listening to the side.

"Hey, I've served with the Lieutenant, I've seen him in action and I know where his loyalties lie. Now button it,

Marine!" growled Spartan.

He turned away from the annoyed marine and looked down at his tactical display. It showed the health and positions of the entire platoon, as well as links to the other marine units in the air and on the ground. He tapped a button and most of the data vanished to show his own platoon and the dangers in their immediate area. The last thing he needed was an information overload in a hostile area.

A great roar rushed from the vessel's engines as they reversed thrust to slow their descent at the very last minute. It was comparable to the kick felt when an aircraft reversed its thrusters when landing.

"Ten seconds!"

The door gunners were already engaging targets but from where Spartan stood he had no idea what they were firing at. The clatter of weapon fire hit the hull of the craft like rain but none of the rounds penetrated, they must have been rifles and pistol ammunition. That was a good start.

They must have hit the ground hard as the seal on the right of the boat holding him upright snapped clean off. It took a superhuman effort on his part not to smash against the bulkhead. As he straightened up, the side door dropped down with a heavy thud and the unit was instantly exposed to the ongoing battle. Without pausing he flicked the seal switch to release his suit and then bounded for the door. The suit was frustratingly slow, no quicker than a man moving at a jogging pace. He went through the doorway and jumped the two-metre drop to the ground scanning the perimeter as he landed. In front were the ruined residential zones that ran out from the outskirts of the city. Most of the buildings were only a few storeys tall but a few were much bigger. A concrete flyover ran from one side to the other, he couldn't see any traffic on it.

Already there were scores of fighters, some marines, some army and many more were volunteers from the city. Most were firing from the windows of buildings, others looked to be running back into the city. A loud noise came from behind and Spartan turned to see his landing craft lift up and then blasted off away from the battlefield. As it moved away the full scale of the battle was revealed to him. Scores of buildings had been demolished. Amongst the rubble dozens of marines were fighting a desperate battle against a great horde of the enemy shock troopers. Mixed in with the bio-engineered soldiers were a number of militia and Zealot fighters. The Zealots were in much smaller numbers than Spartan had expected. Even so, with these enemy numbers he was amazed the defenders had lasted so long.

"Frontline is collapsing, all commando units move to the perimeter and stabilise the line!" came the order.

"First platoon follow me!" Spartan shouted over his radio unit.

The armoured units from his craft moved into a loose line next to him as more arrived into the thick of the action from the other landing craft. But in less than twenty seconds he had enough to start his counterattack. Each of the CES units looked like an armoured monster, bristling with armoured plates, hydraulics and weapons. Spartan moved as quickly as the suit would allow him towards the brutal battle ahead. With the first two-dozen CES units were two platoons of lighter armoured commandos who spread out firing their L48 rifles at any targets they found. The precise rifle fire flicked along the line, as each shot picked off the enemy units one at a time.

The commandos, armed with the assault variants of the L48 provided suppressing fire as the rest moved forward. Spartan reached the rubble first to find three marines fighting one of the shock troopers. One was missing an arm and the other two were desperately stabbing away at the thing with their bayoneted rifles. He pushed past them and slammed his hydraulically powered arm hard into the creature's chest. The strength of the suit was impressive. With one move the creature was knocked back several metres where it crashed into four more of them. As he lifted his right arm he faced them and held down the trigger. Normally the recoil from the L48 rifles would be heavy, but with the weapons mounted directly onto the suit's chassis the unit absorbed the bulk of the recoil. Both weapons fired together bathing the enemy in scores of small but deadly flechette rounds. The creatures were instantly shredded, but many more were moving in to attack.

In the distance Spartan could see the cracks and holes in the ground where the creatures were coming from. It was easy to see why the Air Force had botched up the defence of this segment of the city. By staying underground, the enemy had avoided the bombs and emerged right inside the perimeter of the city. They must have been planning this for months. He turned to the left and then the right, calculating their numbers to be at least two hundred with more still climbing out from the rubble. The rest of the CES units had followed his example. They crashed hard into the enemy line where they had blunted the assault. Great streaks of flame poured from the weapons as they did as much damage as they could as quickly as possible. The lighter armed commandos moved forward and took up positions in the rubble.

Something grabbed at his left leg and as Spartan looked down he saw Lieutenant Daniels approaching. He kicked a creature away before tearing it apart with his linked rifles. Scores of the creatures rushed forward as more continued to crawl out from the rubble. Spartan spotted one trying to get past him and slammed the cutting blade on his left arm into the thing's head. It was neatly slashed off, the body slid down in a mushy mound of gore.

"You okay, Sergeant?" asked Lieutenant Daniels.

Another two creatures leapt at Spartan. Just as they reached within inches of his suit, he pulled the trigger and blasted both of them to shreds of flesh.

"All good here, Sir," Spartan replied as the smoke flittered away.

Fire from a hundred metres away started to hit their positions. One round struck Spartan's visor, jolting him back. As the fire continued most of the commandos and the original defenders dragged themselves behind any cover they could find. Spartan examined the enemy positions ahead and quickly found the dozens of enemy troops firing their weapons. Around these fighters were scores of the shock troops, each one staying low to the ground as the small arms battle continued. One of the troopers stood up and waved something in the air. Spartan tried to get a better view on his display when he saw a smoke trail rushing through the air.

"Get down!" he shouted on the radio.

He looked around but the size of his suit prevented him from doing any more than just lowering himself. The missile struck one of the CES units further down the line and impacted in the centre of its torso. With a great flash the unit exploded, probably aided by the large amounts of ammunition fitted on its back. The explosion and shockwave hit those nearest to it as the smouldering wreckage crashed to the ground.

"Here they come!" Marcus shouted.

From the craters and gaps in the ground a great horde of the enemy climbed up and rushed en masse towards the loose defensive line the marines had established. The charging mass continued to fire their weapons, as they moved more rockets and missiles blasted the line to strike the defenders. The power of the L48 rifles was impressive and each large calibre round stopped a man in his tracks. With the special ammunition they were capable of armour piercing or exploding at set distances. Flashes and bursts ripped from the line as their gunfire did its work.

Spartan locked his armoured feet firmly on the ground, lifted his cutting blade and proceeded to add his own fire to the battle. He was aware of the strengths and limits to the suit but right now he could operate as a stable, armoured fighting platform. Aiming carefully he fired short bursts, each one knocked back two or three hostiles. Some of the enemy had actually made it to the line and he could see several marines stabbing back at them with bayonets as they continued to fire. He fired a long burst along their front line but they kept coming. Two creatures leapt through the air towards him as more appeared at a ruined building to the right. He slashed at the first one and its mutilated body crashed into his armoured head, knocking him backwards. The second one landed on his weapon arm and started to hack at him with a hardened metal weapon that looked like an axe. The impact forced him back and with a grinding screech he collapsed to the floor. As he hit the ground he flailed out with his arms and legs, desperately trying to keep them off him. Five marines rushed over and added their own fire to the action and managed to clear them off Spartan before his suit was torn open. He rolled over and lifted himself up to see the enemy were falling back to cover.

"All unit commanders report in," came the voice on the comms network again.

The audio channels were filled with chatter as each company and platoon commander reported their current status. Spartan noticed that over half the units had been hit hard in that first assault.

"Sergeant, we lost five CES units in that attack. At this rate we'll be out of marines in less than thirty minutes," said Lieutenant Daniels over the secure line.

Spartan was about to reply when an urgent message came in from the monitoring ships in orbit.

"This is General Rivers. We're picking up comms traffic that New Georgia is sending forces to help liberate Carlos from our forces. The other five colonies are still debating but it looks like Avagana is on its own for now. We're sending five companies of reinforcements to the Southern perimeter, ETA forty minutes."

"Lieutenant Daniels here, we need immediate air support, Sir, the front line is fracturing and casualties are heavy!"

"I know, we're monitoring the action from here. They

are throwing everything they have in the South. If you can hold until relieved we will have a chance. I'll have ground support with you in less than ten minutes, good luck, Marines," he said as the radio unit clicked off.

Bullets and missiles continued to pound the line but for now it looked like the enemy were content to pour fire into the defenders, rather than risk another full frontal attack. Though it looked less decisive their greater numbers were slowly taking their toll with the sheer weight of bullets.

"Sir, we have to get out of this fire, we're getting creamed!" Marcus shouted.

Spartan looked around their position, instantly spotting the many dead commandos and a number of the CES units burning or heavily damaged. Another missile streaked across the battlefield and slammed into the arm of a unit, the blast tearing it off but leaving the unit still standing and operational.

"Maybe the suits weren't such a great idea, they're sitting ducks!" said Daniels bitterly.

"You're both right," said Spartan as he quickly assessed the situation. "If we stay here we die. These suits are designed for close-up work, in this kind of firefight we're not going to last long."

"I take it you have a suggestion, Sergeant?"

"Yes, Sir. I suggest the commandos stay here and provide covering fire, the CES units should advance and assault their positions."

"Assault their positions? You mean a full frontal attack against greater numbers?" he asked incredulously.

"Yeah, he's right. We'll be much safer the closer we are to them," Marcus said.

The Lieutenant considered Spartan's proposal, though he knew in his heart that their options were limited. Either they stayed on the line until there was only a handful left, they retreated or they moved forward. If they stayed the enemy would assault them again when their numbers were lowered sufficiently.

"Okay, let's do this!" Daniels said as he checked along the line. He wasn't completely sure it would work but any action was better than waiting to die. He called his units on the tactical net.

"CES units, on my mark you will advance to the enemy, everybody else keep your heads down!"

Two of the units turned to look towards the Lieutenant, surprised at the order to advance in such adverse conditions. Both of them were splattered with blood and scratches ran along the sides of the armour. Lieutenant Daniels suit was painted differently to the rest and distinctively marked with tiger strikes on the lower body. The defending marines kept up a withering fire on the enemy but it was clear a change of tactics was in order. Small groups of the units emerged from what little cover they had found and moved towards open ground. As they prepared for the attack plinks of small arms fire bounced off their thick armour.

"Watch for friendlies out there!" shouted Spartan as he surveyed the assembled platoon.

They looked impressive, each machine a great lump of hardened metal. The battle had already taken its toll and of the entire platoon, only twenty-nine of the armoured suits were still operational. The rest were either destroyed or immobilised.

"Follow me!"

Spartan jumped down from the piled up debris and onto the rough open ground that separated the two sides. As he moved ahead the rest of the ragged line of machines went forward as fast as they could. More rockets and bullets blasted past and a freak missile destroyed at least one unit. Continuing on they fired long bursts to keep the enemies' heads down. Incredibly they made it across the open space with no casualties, although all the suits had sustained a level of damage. Spartan and Daniels hit the enemy front line almost simultaneously. With frenzied savagery they smashed and hacked their way through the shock troops and Zealots alike. As the rest of the platoon arrived it became clear that this was the perfect battleground for the armour. The shouts and screams from both sides were drowned out by grenades and the fire of weapons.

The battle to hold New Carlos was well under way.

CHAPTER THREE

Prometheus was the most unusual and certainly the most dangerous planet in the entire Confederacy. Being the closest planet to the sun it was uninhabitable and no attempts were ever made to sustain life. It was however a rich and valuable source of iron and heavily mined for its resources. Reinforced and shielded ships ploughed their way to the planet and through the Proxima System carrying their wares. What made Prometheus even more deadly though were the terrible storms that forced vessels to take an indirect approach to the fiery world. Risking the storms was tantamount to suicide.

Birth of Prometheus

It was almost midnight on Kerberos yet the lights from the buildings still cast a dull glow across the street and over the nearest buildings. It was a wide road with good access for the many large vehicles that ploughed their way around the colony with their raw materials and goods. At this time of night, when the air became cooler, it could become difficult to breathe. Special Agent Johnson pulled a small cylinder from his pocket and inhaled a mouthful of oxygen. He tried to keep it to a minimum but after all this time waiting outside he was starting to feel the strain. He had been assigned a colonial ATU team for protection and he was acutely aware they were getting tired waiting for something to happen. Normally he would have made use of local police units but this was part of a large operation spread across the city. Officially he worked for Yama's Special Crimes Division but was in fact an agent for the Confederacy's top-secret Naval Intelligence Department. He had been contacted directly by Admiral Jarvis with special orders from Naval Intelligence to keep this operation secret. It had never happened before and therefore told Johnson that this raid was much bigger than anybody realised. He'd left the headquarters two hours ago along with three other teams on similar operations.

Kerberos was becoming a troublesome place with so many companies, organisations, unions and religions all vying for power to the detriment of each other. Even the team he was assigned with had the feel of a group that might just as easily stab him in the back rather than help him. The Confederacy was very important to Johnson. It provided him with a career and a purpose in a troubled part of the colony. Though he kept hearing negative press about the organisation, all he had seen were people trying to help and keep the people safe and secure. Something very big and very important was going on tonight and Johnson was determined he would find out what it was.

One of the street lights flickered and he pulled back into the shadows to keep out of sight. The three other ATU agents with him were each trying to be as discreet as possible. Johnson lowered the night vision on his helmet so he could monitor the movement of their suspects as they moved down the street. The intelligence from their contact said that a new terrorist cell was expected to meet one of the many industrialists on the planet with links to the Zealots. If true it could indicate a growing alliance between important figures on Kerberos and the religious insurgents throughout the Confederacy. The industrialist was already in the club and being watched by their contact, though he was disappointed to find they had no audio or visual feeds into the building.

"Suspect is using his comms gear," came the voice of his contact on the inside.

"Understood," said Johnson quietly.

The team had been waiting for over an hour for this meeting to take place. With the trouble on Prime threatening to travel off-world the success of their mission was even more critical. Johnson was busy thinking about the many different permutations of what was going on when a small black car arrived. It was unmarked and as it stopped outside the building another pulled up behind it. Johnson whispered into his headset.

"Wait, all units hold position."

The door opened and out stepped four men in black suits. They looked like the usual thugs the criminal groups in the city used, but they could equally be legitimate bodyguards for an important dignitary. Three more men exited the second vehicle, each one looked just the same as the previous four. The group spread out, two stayed with the car and the other five moved out to key areas on the street.

"Crap!" muttered Johnson to himself.

As the men fanned out another two people emerged from the second car, one was a man in a light grey business suit, the second a woman wearing an evening dress. The two walked the short distance from the car to the entrance of the bar and went inside.

"Sir, message from Fleet for you," said one of the men as he handed over his communication link.

Johnson lifted the headpiece and tapped the decrypt key on the handset. A series of tones came down the line as the connection was authenticated from his headquarters in the city.

"Special Agent Johnson, this is a recorded message from Admiral Jarvis. Intelligence obtained from the Titan Naval Station indicates several cells on Kerberos. We suspect possible planetary government collusion. I have attached identity ciphers for cleared personnel. Do not share the intelligence you discover on your operation with anyone outside of this circle. Report back to me when you have news, good luck," the voice crackled and then repeated the message.

Johnson looked down at the communication unit and the identity keys it displayed. He pulled out his field datapad, a smaller device than the standard models used in offices, copying the data over. As soon as it completed the recorded message and data associated with it, it was automatically deleted. He removed the headset and handed it back to the security officer.

"Are we going in?" asked one of the officers.

Johnson lifted his hand to signal for them not to move before speaking quietly over the radio system.

"No, we don't move till we get the word from our contact inside," he said firmly before turning back to the surveillance of the building.

"Nobody moves until I give the word!"

* * *

The great hulk of the CCS Crusader pushed on into orbit around Kerberos. Some of her weapon systems were now functional but switched off to conserve power. The last attempt to activate them had shorted out two decks and triggered a series of blasts that took four hours to contain. Most of the bridge staff was helping engineering sections throughout the vessel as they tried to keep the almost crippled vessel in one piece.

On the bridge of the ship Commander Anderson stared out through the virtual windows to survey the planet below. Kerberos was an odd place, a mix of industry, crime and religion. It should have been the perfect place, but money and greed had corrupted the planet more quickly than any had ever expected. It was still a mighty workshop capable of producing anything from computers to starship engines. A small group of gunboats rushed past as they made their way to an unknown objective. He noticed the weapons covering the small craft. They were mighty and just one could cause a real problem to even a warship if given the chance.

Lieutenant Nilsson slammed her hand onto her communication terminal before realising the rest of the command staff was watching her. Lieutenant Carver, the ship's navigator, turned around to see what the noise was before returning to his duties. She sat up straight with a sheepish looking expression on her face. Commander Anderson was busy checking the battle reports from Prime when he heard the fuss.

"Problem, Lieutenant?" he asked with a raised eyebrow.

The officer turned around to face him but she still looked confused.

"While the brute force tools are working, I've been checking on the source of the transmission and also tracked its movement. From the logs the signal did hit us first, but was switched off and then re-activated thirty seconds after we passed."

"So? Maybe they had more data to send?" answered the Commander.

"Maybe. Here's the weird thing though, Sir. If they intended on continuing communication with our ship, why didn't they maintain their target lock with us? I've checked and they didn't redirect their transmission to follow our trajectory."

"It didn't move to track us? Are you positive?"

"Sir, I have tracked the path of the signal and, based on the time of transmission and our course, it is certain they were continuing to transmit at the exact same location."

A few metres away Lieutenant Carver moved several objects on his plotting display. He was busy tracking orbiting objects, ensuring their course wouldn't be interfered with by any debris or unexpected objects. Even though Kerberos was a well establish colony there was always the chance of drifting space junk, discarded satellites, fuel containers or even freak meteors that could spell disaster for any kind of vessel. He had served alongside the Commander in their operations out on the Rim and he had a reputation as an outstanding mathematician. Commander Anderson walked over to him and tapped him on the shoulder. He turned in surprise.

"Commander, sorry, Sir, I didn't see you there."

The Commander pushed his datapad in front of him and showed the path of the signal that led from Kerberos. "Lieutenant, plot me a destination point for the signal, using the time and reference point from this data."

"Sir." The Lieutenant transferred the data from the datapad to his screen. As he moved the information on the screen he scrunched up his face as though something was confusing him. "You know this signal is sending bursts of encoded traffic to a point in the Rim?"

"No, Lieutenant, that is why I asked you to check," answered Anderson sternly.

"Sorry, Sir. I'm calculating the exact trajectory now."

There was a short pause as he checked the ship's navigation system against the latest mapping details. On the screen he displayed a two dimensional chart with the planet of Kerberos on the left and the beam rushing off to the right. First it moved through where their ship had been, then it continued out of the planet's orbit and out further into the System.

"Apart from us it is aimed at nothing else in orbit. Tracking it further through the system..." he said, as the beam kept moving.

The chart zoomed out as the beam moved further and further until the millions of bodies in the Rim appeared. The beam entered the outer section of the Rim and stopped.

"The Rim?" he asked to himself.

"Makes sense, Commander," said Lieutenant Nilsson who was watching from her screen.

"Thank you, Carver, as you were." The Commander turned and walked back to Lieutenant Nilsson, who was checking her own data on the Rim. Once the Commander was close enough she spoke quietly.

"The signal must have been intended for somebody or some group in the Rim."

"But who? The Rim isn't fully charted. It's a mixture of asteroids, mining stations, refineries and space stations. Is there any way of getting a more precise location from the source of the signal?"

"No, Sir, the best I can manage is the Alpha Three segment of the Rim, but that still includes over three thousand space bodies. It could even be a ship out there," she said.

"Maybe the signal is routine?"

"Routine with a narrow band encoded transmission? I don't think so, Sir. The only people with the equipment for that kind of long range transmission is the Confed Navy or one of the main government departments on Kerberos. If it was military traffic, it would be sealed with the standard ciphers so that only our own command staff could access it. I think it much more likely it was sent by someone else. It can't be a coincidence that the encoding is much stronger than used for civilian traffic, yet is not using military ciphers. My opinion is that this is either important military data to somebody that doesn't want to be found or, more likely that somebody on Kerberos is communicating with a group out on the Rim and they don't want anybody else knowing about it."

Commander Anderson checked the log as he examined the route taken by the beamed transmission. He was all too familiar with the Rim and the complexity of finding even a base or ship, let alone an individual person. It was known through the Proxima System that if you wanted to disappear or renege on a deal you would hide out in the Rim, as you would never be found. The downside was that it was crawling with unsavoury characters that were usually best avoided. Until he had more information it would be useless trying to investigate this further.

"Okay, good work, Lieutenant. Let me know when you have more data on the decryption. Keep this between us."

As Lieutenant Nilsson continued her work on the encrypted data packet the damaged vessel continued its plodding course to the shipyards over Kerberos.

* * *

The light flashed on Johnson's communicator, it was the signal that the target was in position. He took a deep breath and then gave the hand signal to move in. At first nothing happened, it was as if none of the men were ready, but in fact it was the adrenalin kicking in and slowing the burst of activity. His unit fanned out as the spotters and their snipers took out the guards in the street with tranquiliser slugs. The shots were accurate and in less than two seconds the street was clear and the entry team rushed across the street. Johnson was second at the door waiting to the side as two armoured ATU men moved into assault positions. With a flicker the fanned-out metal shields extended from their armour to provide additional protection. They stepped a small distance apart to give the third man space to wield his ram. It was a heavy tool and contained a built in pneumatic pump that could smash through almost any door. With a low thump it smashed the exterior door from its hinges and the way was clear.

"Go, go, go!" shouted Johnson.

The two at the front went in quickly, each carrying a thermal shotgun at the ready. The orders were to avoid hostilities if possible, but in these situations it could easily turn violent. These weapons were deadly at close range but wouldn't break through the outer walls and possibly injure innocent bystanders. Johnson followed closely behind them with his pistol drawn and at the ready. The hallway was dark, the only lighting from red strip lights running along the ceiling. A loud throbbing beat from the sound system made normal discussion almost impossible. As they reached the end of the hallway they came to the door that led to the staircase. It went up to the second floor and into the main dance floor and club. Sat in a kiosk to the right was a scantily clad woman, presumably there to take cash from the patrons. She grabbed something from the wooden unit to her side and swung it around at the ATU officers. The first managed to dodge out of the way but the second took a direct blast from the firearm. Johnson jumped to grab her arm. With a hard pull he smashed her hand on the unit and the pistol dropped to the floor. More ATU officers arrived and one of them secured her with manacles escorting her out of the building.

Johnson checked his map on his small datapad. According to the data sent by his contact the suspect was thirty metres across the dance floor, sat at a round table and flanked by two guards. He nodded to his men and without waiting they went up the staircase and towards the wide glass entrance leading into the dance hall. As they reached the last few steps Johnson pulled out his pistol.

"Non-lethal," he whispered over the radio system.

The two armoured officers checked their weapons were set to the low power settings before indicating they were ready.

From the glass doorways they could see the lights moving about but it was impossible to see what else was happening.

"Go!" said Johnson.

The first officer pushed the door slightly open and

then tossed a stun grenade inside. As soon as it reached the centre of the room it flashed. The pulse was strong and would incapacitate anybody in the room. Without waiting the three were inside the dance hall, but it was quickly obvious something was very wrong. There were no dancers and the only people in the room were already on the floor, face down as though they had been told to get down. Johnson ran to the table to find his contact slumped across the table with his datapad smashed on the ground.

"Shit!"

The rest of the team moved in and secured the area, each checking for signs of the suspect.

"Sir, blood!" called one of the officers as he pointed out a dark trail running out to the side of the room and stopped at a wall.

"Get that music off!" shouted Johnson as he examined the wall. He tapped his pistol and could easily tell it wasn't thick. Pulling it back he struck the wall and the pistol smashed through the thin layers. Pushing his hand into the hole he found he could slide the section of wall to the side. It revealed a messy room full of smashed computer terminals and papers. He was about to enter when a man in a suit appeared from behind a stack of machines and opened fire with an old fashioned shotgun.

Johnson's reactions were only just quick enough to save him but the ATU officer behind took the full brunt in the chest, flying back two metres before crashing down hard. Johnson leaned around the gap and fired three rounds at the man but he had already vanished. From his position Johnson could see the window was open and outside were the rusty metal railings of the fire escape.

"Fire escape!" he shouted and ran into the room to give chase.

As he reached the ledge the man was already down the first part of the metal staircase. He fired a shot to try and make him stop. There was no way the man was going to wait though and he kept moving. Johnson squeezed himself out of the window and onto the iron gantry that led to the staircase. As he rushed down the steps he could make out the shape of the man below.

"In pursuit of suspect, I need the fire escape cut off, block the street. He is armed and prepared to use force!"

The suspect was crouching near the ledge and as Johnson emerged he fired a blast of lead shot that managed to catch his right leg. It was a near miss but a few of the tiny pieces of lead managed to take chunks from the close fitting armour he wore under his suit and made him lose his balance. With a flailing action he tried to grab the railing but it was too little too late. He crashed down and rolled down three steps. Johnson looked up to see then man, he was dark skinned and had serpent like tattoos on his cheeks. The man lifted the shotgun and pointed it at Johnson.

"No, wait!" he shouted but the man didn't hesitate, he pulled the trigger but nothing happened other than the click of the hammer.

The man muttered and then turned to continue his run to the bottom of the fire escape. Johnson lifted himself up but the pain in his back and legs told him the fall had hurt him more than expected. He heard shouting and leaned out over the side to see the man running across the lane. Taking careful aim he pointed the weapon low and squeezed off two shots. The first missed but the second struck the man above the knee.

"Suspect is down, where are you?" shouted Johnson into his radio gear.

He supported his weight on the metal railings and moved the last few steps to the ground below. In the darkness it wasn't easy to focus in the shadows. He paused for a second to take a quick gasp of oxygen, the last rush had really taken it out of him. He then went over to the slow moving body of the suspect.

"Freeze!" He lowered his pistol and pointed it at the man's head.

The man stopped and rolled over to look directly into Johnson's face, the pain from the wound was evidently becoming worse. He grabbed for a concealed blade but Johnson was ready for that and quickly kicked it away. The agent knelt down next to him and put pressure on the wound.

"I want..." he said before noticing the frothing at the man's mouth.

He grabbed at the man and tried to force out whatever was there but it was too late. In just seconds the poison had done its work and the man lay dead. Johnson slumped down next to the body, the raid had failed and their suspect was dead. There was still no sign of his backup and that was starting to worry him. He looked over to the body of the man, noticing the tattoos again. They were the mark of the secretive Church of Echidna, an organisation that was connected to the Zealots and attacks throughout the System. He checked the man's pockets but found nothing other than some shells for his weapon. He pulled back the jacket reaching down to the trouser pocket only to find a pouch on the man's belt. Johnson instantly recognised the feel.

"Datapad!" He pulled out the valuable electronic device. Holding it in front of him he ran his finger along the top to activate the unit. With a flicker of light blue text it powered up and waited with some kind of icon-based security panel. Then he heard footsteps.

"About dammed time!" he said as he looked up from the body.

The shape in the distance was of a man in a long coat and wearing a wide brimmed hat. The man was coming towards him, then he realised he was pointing a weapon. Jumping back he avoided the blast from the man's pistol.

Then he was gone. Johnson gave chase but his back and leg were still causing him pain.

"Special Agent Johnson, in pursuit of shooter. He's coming around to the side street. Where are you?" he shouted.

The man disappeared through a dark archway in the wall that led to a courtyard at the side of the main building. He approached the arch area with care and popped his head inside then back out, it looked clear. Keeping his pistol raised he slipped through the arch to find an empty courtyard.

"What the hell?" He angrily keyed the radio again, "Johnson here, what's going on?"

There was a crackle followed by one of the ATU agents. "We're in the alley, where is the body?"

Johnson shook his head, he simply couldn't believe the incompetence of these men he had been assigned. He gave one last look to the courtyard and then turned back though the arch and into the alley. As he moved closer he could see three of the ATU men, all stood in their armour with their weapons ready for danger. He approached the first who stood waiting for him.

"He was right here!"

The man looked down then back to Johnson. "Maybe he was just wounded and got away?"

The second officer stepped closer. "Did you find anything?" he asked.

Johnson looked at him, something was clearly wrong with this situation. Not least, because all three of the ATU men had their hands on their shotguns and looked ready to shoot. He instantly felt nervous and decided to take no chances.

"Nothing, this raid was a disaster! Let's get back to Headquarters, I've got paperwork to file," he said angrily.

As the officers turned to return to the street Johnson noticed a look of satisfaction between the two of the men. He pushed his hand inside his armoured jacket, checking the recovered datapad was still there. He was right, there was definitely something suspicious going on and he was going to find out what it was, wherever the evidence took him.

* * *

Teresa finished her lunch and pushed the tray to one side. From where she sat she could look out through the windows to the planet below. Well, in reality she was looking at the wall as the computer systems were set to replicate the exterior view on the walls of the secure section inside the rotating section of the ship. As she looked out at the planet of Prime below she could see specks of grey as the Fleet sent more vessels to the surface. In the last hour she had counted over a hundred craft heading down from the transports and capital ships of the Navy that were scattered around the planet. One of the transit stations was already being used as a drop off point for materials and supplies for the war effort. She was ever amazed at the speed and ingenuity shown by the armed forces when facing a crisis.

Unlike the operation on the moon of Kronus a few days before, the combat operations around Prime were now no longer just the domain of the Marine Corps. The heavy transports of the Confederate Army had now arrived. Though their numbers were much greater than those of the marines they were normally used for static garrisons, security operations or for bulking up the numbers in major combat operations. The fact they had arrived signalled a change in the campaign and not one for the good. The Army was notorious for its poor discipline and corruption in the Officer Corps, well, that was what she had heard anyway. From what she had seen on the intelligence reports being sent around the ship they were going to need every soldier and marine they could find to keep Prime under control. If that meant making use of the Army so be it. The Marine Corps could hardly be expected to do all the work, there were only so many of them.

The canteen was much quieter than normal with the marines busy fighting down on the surface. She was still fuming at her visit an hour earlier in the medical bay. She had originally been told she would be able to report back for duty in a couple of days, but it seemed the surgeon had botched the work and most of it had been redone. The damage wasn't life threatening but the bullet impacts could have caused long-term damage without the operations. The extra work meant she couldn't return to her unit for combat operations for at least another forty-eight hours until the stitches had healed. The medical bay was well equipped and rather than having to wait weeks for the wounds to heal she needed a matter of hours for the process to start. It still felt too long and the thought of her comrades fighting when she was stuck in orbit was driving her stir crazy. It wasn't that she was desperate for battle or was trying to contain some kind of bloodlust. She just hated being on her own on a new ship, with few people she knew and nothing to do. She and Spartan had spent months on the marine ship CCS Santa Maria as they completed their basic training. Her new posting was essentially the same but there were enough differences for her to feel uncomfortable.

Two marines from the Signals Unit walked past with towels draped over their shoulders. As with all the marines on the ship they were expected to keep themselves fit, both mentally and physically. Maybe a bit of physical exercise would help.

"Hey, you off to the gym?" she asked.

"Yeah, time for some sparring," said the first man.

The second man turned to her. "You wanna join us?"

He quickly noticed the bandages just showing along her collar. "Sorry, I didn't know you were injured, you take a hit or something?"

"Yeah, on the landing at Titan, took a few rounds in the arm." She stretched the injured limb.

The two men sat down facing her and quickly introduced themselves.

"I'm Corporal Kowalski, this is Private Bishop, we just arrived with the new recruits from boot camp on Carthago."

"Teresa Morato."

She looked at the two men, noting they were both in their thirties and had the assuredness she'd seen on the more experienced marines on the ship. Bishop had a dark tattoo running down the side of his face and disappeared into his tunic.

"You're not recruits though, right?"

"Hell no," replied Bishop. "We're part of the Guard Unit down on Carthago but we were transferred nine months ago to come to the Proxima System. We heard it was supposed to be the new paradise!"

"Hell, they got that wrong!" laughed Kowalski. "We've been training rookies for the last nine months and were supposed to be transferring to Kerberos when our taskforce arrived here. Instead most of us were sent to Prime to help with the siege down there."

Teresa said nothing, her mind obviously elsewhere. She

gazed at them before realising they were waiting for her to speak.

"I, uh, my family is from Carthago," she mumbled.

"I thought Carthago citizens weren't allowed to join up because of the troubles?" Kowalksi asked.

"My family helped the Confed resistance so I was given an exemption to serve to pay my family's debts," she said bitterly.

"What do you mean?" asked Bishop.

Teresa said nothing and it was clear the subject was one she didn't want to continue. The two marines sat uncomfortably before Bishop broke the silence.

"Isn't that where they reckon the Church of Echidna got started back with the early colonies?"

Kowalski shrugged and pulled out his datapad. He brought up several pages on the Church and its early history.

"Says here the Church was founded by some of the early colonists from Earth. They were a kind of minority monotheistic cult that suffered a schism which turned violent. After the Great War they scattered through the Systems, with many of them going on the long voyage to the new colonies in Proxima. Apparently they tried to unify their church with the colonial governments but were forced to stop. Since then parts of the more conservative wings of the church have broken away to continue the fight with violence while the rest preach peace and tolerance."

"Tolerance my ass!" laughed Bishop. "Did you join up at Carthago then?"

Teresa turned her head in disagreement as she remembered what had happened. The memories were still fresh, the long drawn out illness of her husband and her years of work trying to earn enough money in the poverty stricken world of Carthago. She looked up and Bishop and answered though her voice was slower and obviously upset.

"No, I joined a mining operation out near Prometheus."

"Prometheus? That's the new colony on the fire world. Hell, that's the closest planet to the sun right?"

"That's wild. I've heard that place is rough. Aren't most of the stations there full of strip bars and underground arenas?" asked Kowalski.

"Yeah, something like that. It's where Spartan and I were volunteered for training. It takes a long time to get to Prometheus, why do you think so much illegal activity goes on out there? If you avoid the storms and stop at Agora and Hydra like we did, it takes nearly thirty weeks journey just to get back to Prime."

"I've been thinking of spending some of my vacation leave there, but the trip is too long. Isn't there a faster way?" Bishop asked.

"I've heard a direct trip avoiding the storms can be done in about half that, but if the storms kick up you'll have to wait for a gap. Might be days but sometimes months. You can risk running the storms but apparently half the ships that try it are destroyed, if you make it through then it can be done in less than a week." Kowalski explained.

Bishop rested one had on his face as he listened. Then it dawned on him.

"Wait a sec, Teresa, did you say you were on Kronus, during the siege?"

"Yeah, you could say that. We'd only just finished basic and got sent on our first operation," she said with a grimace.

"No way! I've been in the Marine Corps for more than six years and never even drawn a pistol in anger. You get here as a rookie and they throw you into the fire. I heard it was rough down there. A few guys from our unit were on one of the transit stations during the battle."

"Did you see any of the Zealots while you were there?" asked Kowalski.

"Forget that, man, have you seen any of their super soldiers?" Bishop interrupted.

"Super soldiers? You mean the bio-engineered shock troopers they are using?" she asked with a crooked smile. "No. A friend of mine called Spartan was on a boarding action with a small team when they found the first of them."

"The ship that tried to escape from the Victorious, right? We were told that unit got pretty messed up," Kowalski said.

"Yeah, when they got back they showed me the video feeds from the boarding action. Those things are evil. I don't know how they created them but they are faster and stronger than anything I've seen before."

Teresa leaned back to stretch, she hadn't exercised for two days and her muscles were starting to feel it. At least now she had somebody to talk to. It was the most interesting thing that had happened since the marines had returned to Prime.

"I don't want to sound rude, but if you've only just completed basic, how the hell did you get on the Santa Cruz? You know this is a commando ship now, right?"

"You don't say, Bishop. A few of us had already completed most of the commando training before we landed on Kronus. The unit I was with was involved in the frontal assault of the station. Apparently a lot of the commando units took heavy casualties in the first waves. They started picking a few from each unit to make up the numbers."

"So marine to commando in less than a week, nice going!"

"How about you two, Bishop?"

"What do you mean?"

"Well, I assume you're going to the surface?"

"Yeah. As soon as the next wave of landing craft is ready we'll be going down to the surface. The LT said we've got about ten hours for the boats to be repaired and loaded for the next run."

The whistle indicating the start of the next watch on the ship caught their attention. The two marines looked around the canteen, noting they were the only ones still there.

"We'd better get to the gym before chow," said Kowalski as he stood up from the table. "Nice talking to you, we'll see you around I hope."

Teresa went to join them but the pain struck hard and fast in her shoulder. "Bitch!" she swore and staggered off to her quarters.

CHAPTER FOUR

The Confederate Navy Fighter Wings were the elite fighting arm of the Navy and contained the best trained pilots in the Fleet. Though most squadrons were based at the Naval bases and battlegroups around Terra Nova a few squadrons did play their part in the Proxima Emergency. Operating from escort cruisers and carriers the men and women of the Fighter Wings made use of the two most advanced craft in the Fleet. The MK II Lightning twin-engine interceptor and the Thunderbolt MK I a four-engine torpedo bomber with enough firepower to cripple a frigate.

Thunder and Lightning

Marcus had already been forced to abandon his CES suit due to damage sustained in a rocket attack on the front line. With the armour now stacked along with other damaged or unused ordnance, he was forced to duck for cover as a mortar shell exploded nearby. He still wore his Personal Defence Suit but, compared to the thick metal armour he'd previously worn, he now felt naked to the enemy fire that clattered about their defensive positions.

"Sniper!" shouted one of the marines from the outer wall.

Marcus was already in a foxhole when the first round hit, it managed to miss him by just a few centimetres. Dirt and chipped stone smashed against his armour but thankfully the thin armoured sections easily brushed off the impact.

"Thank the Gods!" he whispered to himself as he held his body down low. The civilians would find this kind of combat far more gruelling, as they had almost no armour of any kind. Even loose debris was causing them problems, let alone the artillery fire from the enemy. More shots flicked past and he winced as a large calibre bullet whipped close to him and embedded in a nearby wall. The battle had altered from a grinding full-scale assault to one of sniping and rocket attacks, where every few minutes screams and shouting indicated yet another person had been hurt or killed.

The city of New Carlos was coming to the end of its fifth day in the siege, yet the damage all around suggested it had been like this for weeks, maybe even months. What had started as a bloodthirsty hand-to-hand battle around the outer suburbs of the city had now pushed pack into the commercial spaces, where the larger buildings and road systems provided ample cover for friend or foe alike. It was here the new defensive line had been erected, built upon the blood of the commandos and marines who had given their lives to buy enough time for the defences to be built.

Spartan and the surviving commandos took cover behind the concrete and debris the citizens and engineers had spent the last six hours preparing. It was rough but the marines had done their job and given the city time to prepare a perimeter that was capable of standing, at least for the short term. The enemy had not assaulted the line for almost an hour and the defenders were not wasting a minute of it. Holes in the ground were quickly converted to slit trenches while bricks, dirt and debris were made into mounts and cover from fire.

With the commandos helping to guard the perimeter defences, Spartan and other still working CES units had help demolish the smaller buildings to create additional cover. Right now he was near what used to be a small office complex that had already been occupied by a score of volunteers from the city. They were keen but had almost no idea what they were doing. Still, they were better than nothing. The effect of the citizens doing their part was proving to be a great boost to the morale of the beleaguered city.

Marcus climbed out of his foxhole and rushed the short distance across the open ground till he reached the concrete parking structure the commandos were using as a reasonably secure forward base. As he reached its relative safety, he dropped down next to Spartan who was out of his CES and smoking a cigarette.

"You need to keep your head down," Spartan laughed.

"Really? Yeah, thanks for that."

Two more marines settled near them, one a dark skinned veteran called Tex who was recruited from one of the many gangs on Prometheus, the other a moody looking corporal, Travis.

"Spartan, a few of the guys said you were from Prometheus too. How did they get you to join up?" asked Tex.

Marcus jumped in as Spartan continued to smoke, enjoying the break from the backbreaking labour of the recent fighting.

"You're from Prometheus and you haven't heard of Spartan?" asked Marcus with feigned surprise.

"The only Spartan I know of was a cop killer, that ain't you, right?" he answered with a sly grin.

Marcus looked over to Spartan nervously, knowing of his background and propensity to rely on brute force to resolve the most basic of issues. There was no response from him. It was as if he hadn't heard a word.

"Spartan ain't no cop killer. He was on the fighting circuit when the place got busted. You know, the clampdown raids from almost a year ago."

"Shit, man, he was in the raids? My group got busted at the same time!" said Tex.

Spartan turned to look at him. Tex moved closer but Spartan stared into his eyes blowing a puff of smoke into the man's face.

"I never saw the fighting circuit, I thought it was all underground shit on Prometheus?" asked Travis, now intrigued by the whole conversation.

"Spartan here was the champion in nearly a dozen fights, weren't you?" Marcus placed his hand on Spartan's shoulder.

The rattle of anti-aircraft weapons pulled their attention away to the horizon where streaks of tracer fire raced up into the sky. A wing of four Thunderbolt fighter bombers screeched overhead, each craft leaving a light grey trail of smoke behind it. The aircraft had deployed their wings and weapon pods for atmospheric flight and looked deadly from this distance. Pale yellow streaks indicated the automatic cannons of the aircraft were strafing the insurgent positions outside the boundaries of the city.

"Army aircraft?" Spartan asked.

"Yeah, the ground pounder must be on the way." Marcus was watching the aircraft move off into the distance.

Spartan flicked the ash from the end of his cigarette as he took one long puff then dropped the stub to the floor. His helmet was off but he was still in his standard Personal Defence Suit. There wasn't a chance he'd be caught without any armour. So many of the wounded had suffered their injuries from rubble and shrapnel.

"Look!" shouted one of the other marines sitting on a ruined wall.

They saw a line of yellow flashes in the distance. A few seconds later a crump of exploding napalm bombs washed over their defences.

"Yep, it's the Army alright!" said Marcus.

"And they thought we were subtle!" Spartan laughed as he stood up.

He moved over towards where his CES armour was leaning against the wall. It was now scratched and dented on almost every section. The visor had a centimetre long crack along the left side where a missile fragment had struck him. He pushed his feet down inside the unit, the armour adjusted and began clamping down around him. This was the part that Spartan always hated. No matter how many times he was reassured by the engineers and artificers, there was always the possibility that the armour could continue its movement and crush the body or limbs of the marine inside. Apparently it had never happened but that didn't alter the way Spartan felt. He pushed his back into the suit and took a deep breath.

"Here goes nothing," he said quietly.

As his back touched the metal a series of whining

motors pushed the metal and rubber mounts up to link and interface with his PDS suit. It took less than twenty seconds before the entire unit was clamped around his body and encased him in heavy metal. Next to him Marcus was halfway through the same procedure when they noticed a small group of commandos approaching.

The three at the front of the group were wearing CES suits and Spartan instantly recognised the paint scheme of his commanding officer.

"Sergeant!" shouted Lieutenant Daniels as he examined the high ground along their position.

"Sir?"

"Get a squad up there with heavy weapons. How is the perimeter looking? Any sign of them?"

Spartan moved his eyes to select options on his communication gear so he could speak with his squad commanders. The bulk of the suit was controlled using the built-in head display and the controls fitted inside the arms. Most of the suit was powered up but it took a few seconds for all the system to kick in. A few lights flickered and then settled, but he noted he had two warnings on the hydraulic levels for the left arm. He'd already had it checked by the unit's artificer and there was nothing they could do until he was back at a fully equipped repair shop. Still, the last thing he needed was for one of his limbs to seize up in battle.

"Corporal Thomas, put your squad on top of the office

complex. Establish an observation post and get some heavy weapons up there." He turned back to Daniels. "Sir, the perimeter is looking solid. We have linked up with the rest of General Shears' forces on our right flank."

Daniels approached him, his armoured suit now starting to grind as the wear of combat and constant use was have an adverse affect on the moving parts. Spartan could see a small number of people at the highest position on the outer wall. The wall was built around a partially demolished housing block now covered in mounted machineguns and mortars. Right in the centre was a large battle standard of one of the cities militia units. It contained the emblem of the city, the Purple of the Confederacy. There were at least twenty small holes punched through it where enemy fire had ripped into the fabric, yet it still stood tall and bright. It was a sign to everyone that this part of the line was secure and held not just by the military but by citizens of New Carlos itself. Daniels stopped in front of him, his armoured torso grinding to a halt. He looked back at the flag and then to Spartan.

"I don't understand, they've been hitting us for hours, why aren't they attacking the line now?"

Spartan checked the tactical display in his suit. It wasn't as detailed as the information you would expect to find in a command centre, but it did show a physical map of the terrain and colours markers for all known friendly and hostile units. He examined the enemy's dispositions before replying to the Lieutenant.

"Well, based on their last two attacks, I'd say they're looking for another way in. The last attack was a disaster for them, Sir. Maybe they are waiting for darkness?"

"Perhaps." The Lieutenant rechecked their position. "I don't like it. We have a strong defensive line here but not much of a reserve. What if they are working out a way to go over or under our lines?"

"They could have access to more tunnels, Sir?" suggested Spartan.

"We should probably get some of the tech teams from the General's staff to do a full subterranean survey of the city. Good plan, Sergeant. In the meantime assemble a small group, a mixture of CES, commandos and anybody else you can find. Set up a reserve outpost back there, on the overpass." He pointed at the raised roadway half a kilometre away. "If anyone tries anything I want to make sure we have someone I can depend on when it goes to hell!"

"Sir!"

Spartan understood the well-hidden complement the officer had made. How intentional it was he had no idea. Spartan looked back at the front line and the scores of people carrying rubble, supplies and ammunition. Even though there was an obvious lull in the battle, it could end at any time. He was secretly glad for a few minutes respite from the frontline where so many marines had already been picked off in the fighting and where he knew another attack was imminent.

* * *

In high orbit above the surface of Prime was the Confederate Fleet, recently bolstered by a dozen newly arrived small frigates helping to reinforce the ever growing blockade around the planet. Streams of transports transferred their cargos to the transit stations before returning on their long voyages to the refineries, military bases and outposts of the Confederacy. Smaller craft made the dangerous trip through the thick atmosphere of Prime to deliver people, supplies and weapons to those on the ground. The most recent arrival was the heavy armoured transports of the Army, with their own frigates providing escort.

The most powerful vessel remaining at the blockade was the CCS Wasp, commanded by Captain Hardy. Though he commanded the ship it was now the home of the battlegroup and Admiral Jarvis had transferred her flag aboard, following the evacuation of the Crusader for emergency repairs at Kerberos.

Wasp was nothing as intimidating as one of the Confederation battleships but she was still a mighty vessel, bristling with weapons and carrying a variety of combat craft. Deep inside the armoured hull of the ship Admiral Jarvis, now accompanied by General Rivers, stood around the tactical display as they examined the situation on Avagana.

Throughout the CiC the dozen officers monitored communication channels and data traffic as they helped coordinate the massive operation on the ground and in space. The tactical map showed an updated model of the planet's surface and the ongoing operations. One of the displays crackled and the image of General Shears appeared. He was in charge of the combined ground based forces of Prime, though with the disputes in the colonies most of his forces had now evacuated to Avagana.

"Admiral," said the old General as he straightened himself at the sight of his opposite number.

General Rivers, the overall commander of ground operations in the sector moved closer so that he appeared next to the Admiral.

"General, what is the situation in New Carlos?" asked General Rivers.

General Shears looked at the Marine Corps officer with disdain. Though they were both senior officers there had always been a level of disagreement between planetary colonial forces and the space based Confederate Marine forces. The rivalry often spilled into spats between officers.

"The city is secure, for now. I have deployed forces to the city perimeter and have established a command centre and reserve deployment area at the Space Port."

"And the rest of Avagana?" asked Rivers.

"Only one city was fully overrun, my colonial forces are dealing with that problem. Right now I'm more concerned with the garrisons throughout the Seven Colonies. The last signal from Fort Wellington was that rebel forces had surrounded the fort and were demanding their surrender."

"Yes, we've been monitoring the situation from up here. The city defence forces and some of the army units are not responding to our signals right now. We suspect some may have been infiltrated or attacked," said Admiral Jarvis.

There was a long pause from the General, as he spoke quietly to somebody off camera, then turned back to the camera.

"My forces are loyal, if you are unable to contact them it is because somebody is jamming them. What about my reinforcements?" he said angrily.

General Rivers looked less than impressed with the response from the General.

"Listen, General Shears, we have three divisions of infantry preparing for combat landings. One is being dropped to the West of New Carlos. They are being landed along with armour and close air support. The other two will help secure the East Coast and the cities between there and New Carlos."

Admiral Jarvis checked her computer display for the progress of the Army transports. From her figures they were about an hour away from starting their operations.

"How does that help me?" demanded General Shears,

"I need more men for the defence of the city!"

"No, General. You must hold with what you have. The Army has the numbers and firepower to clear the open ground. Watch the perimeter and hold. We anticipate Army forces will link up with New Carlos in approximately seventy-two hours," Rivers explained.

The man lowered his head in disagreement then cut the signal.

"Well, he's a pleasant fellow," said a grinning Admiral Jarvis.

"I don't like it." General Rivers looked worried. "He has a reputation for being a bit of a hot head and he really doesn't like the idea of regular army units stealing his glory for retaking Avagana."

"What do you think he will do?"

"I don't know but you can be sure it won't be well thought out. Can you get back to him?"

With a gesture from Jarvis the communications officer walked over and saluted.

"I need to speak to General Shears again, urgently!"

The man saluted and moved back to his console. He hit a number of buttons as he tried to break through the jamming coming from the surface.

"Sir, we are being jammed from the source, I can't burn through to New Carlos or the General," he said apologetically.

Movement caught her eye as she looked out through the

virtual windows on the walls. The glint of light had come from the column of six heavy infantry transports of the Army. They each carried thousands of soldiers as well as scores of tanks and ground support aircraft. The hangar doors were already open and the mechanical loading gear was pushing out the huge Landers that would deposit the men one company at a time. Each one looked like a large ant with their multiple sections and large legs that were currently folded away prior to re-entry through the atmosphere. They would deploy the legs as they landed.

Another of the massive Army ships was releasing a dozen strike aircraft. These machines were based on the shuttles used by the marines but were optimised for high-speed close air support. The craft contained a crew of a dozen personnel to operate the myriad of weapon mounts and missile systems. The largest of all the craft was the Assault Lander, a large vehicle that had all of its transport capacity removed and replaced by batteries of artillery and heavy guns mounted along one side of the craft. As it pushed away from the transport its engines fired up pushing the Lander into a lower orbit prior to its landing.

Although the Navy had the bulk of the ships, the Army operated the planetary defence forces which included a small fleet of transports and light escorts. Many battles were fought over who was responsible for different operations, the Army trying to wrestle control of orbital bombardment and support, with the Navy maintaining the long range ships and assault troops of the Confederation. All warships were under the command of the Navy, much to the annoyance of the Army commanders. This was a consequence of the events during the Great War.

General Rivers moved up alongside her and watched the flotilla.

"It's a wondrous thing watching the Army deploy," he said with a hint of amusement.

"Indeed. They move at a snail's pace but when they do arrive they hit like a ton of bricks. They won't know what's hit them," replied the Admiral.

She didn't look terribly impressed at the sight of the monstrous vessels unloading their military cargos. The arrival of the Army would also mean the involvement of petty squabbles and politics. She would much rather the simple command and control of Navy in space and Marines on the ground. It was never going to be that simple though she thought to herself.

"Admiral, I will need to coordinate this action." He turned smartly to rejoin his combat staff that were already plotting the landing sites and targets to strike.

Admiral Jarvis stayed at her post as she continued to track the progress of the Fleet. The number of vessels in orbit around the planet was growing by the day but there were still gaps in the line and vessels could break through with enough speed if they timed it right. Since the Station had been retaken, over thirty attempts had been made for various craft to break orbit. Most were transports carrying refugees but three had been suicide craft and one had even been loaded with a full complement of the shock troopers.

"I'm picking up movement from low orbit. Medium sized transport, ETA twelve minutes," said the tactical weapons officer.

The officer hit a key on his terminal as he checked the configuration of the vessel. It didn't take him long to find the correct ship in the database and in seconds he had crosschecked it with Confed Naval records.

"Sir, it's an Icarus Class medium transport, she's heading right for us!"

Captain Hardy moved to the centre of the bridge. The Admiral commanded the Fleet, but it was still his ship and he knew how to get the most out of his crew. Jarvis nodded as he carried on.

"Are they showing on IFF?"

"Negative, Sir, there are no transmissions coming from the vessel. They are still accelerating."

The IFF system was the Identify Friend of Foe system that was a requirement of every vessel, be it civilian or military. Each time a craft made a journey its logs and codes were updated. This allowed customs and military forces to establish the origins and allegiance of a vessel when at range. It might seem draconian, but with the kind of distances the ships passed it wasn't always possible to easily identify a craft before it was too late.

Hardy turned around and wiped his forehead.

"Admiral, I recommend full alert, this craft could cripple any one of our ships. If they hit the transports we'll lose thousands!"

"The transports, how do they know?" Without waiting for an answer the Admiral pulled the intercom close to her mouth.

"Action stations! We have incoming craft! Set Condition Red through the Fleet. All ships have permission to open fire on unidentified vessels within twenty kilometres!"

"Where is our CAP?" she asked.

"Combat Air Patrol is already on a course to intercept, they will be in range in sixty seconds," said one of the officers.

"Put me on with the lead pilot."

With a few clicks of the buttons Admiral Jarvis was on with the pilot of the closing fighter. On the screen in front of her the data for the Lightning MK II Fighter appeared. It was a small two-man craft equipped with automatic cannons and anti-ship missiles. The Lightning Fighters were carried aboard many of the carriers in the Fleet, as well as some of the escort cruisers where a few small craft were handy for use in customs duties or ship defence.

"Lieutenant Jacobs, Fourth Interceptor Wing, closing on unidentified craft."

"This is Admiral Jarvis. Are you detecting any signs of life or any transmissions coming from the craft?"

There was a short pause punctuated by the crack and hiss of static. The officers in the CiC of the Wasp kept quiet, each waiting for the word.

"Admiral, the vessel is already damaged, she's leaking fuel and it looks like the port hull has been shredded by anti-aircraft fire. She was hit trying to get from the surface, I can't tell who did the shooting though."

"I need to know if it is a threat. Can you see inside the craft?"

The pause was much longer this time and as she waited, Admiral Jarvis looked over to General Rivers. He had already helped plan the dispersal of the ground forces from the first transport but many more were unloading and they were right in the path of the craft.

"I can see inside. The passenger section is full of containers of some kind. Can't quite tell from here," there was a pause before he continued, "there is nobody at the helm, I repeat there..." he said but the transmission was mysteriously cut off.

"Damn!" growled Captain Hardy. "Who else is out there?" he demanded.

The weapons officer checked the rest of the approaching units but could find no one who could reach the vessel before it was in range of the Fleet. He cycled through the attack wing. The nearest ship was too far away to fire its weapons, but they might be able to get a visual. He sent a coded signal to the leading fighter's computer receiving an acknowledgement and video feed almost immediately. As the video popped up the pilot of the vessel spoke.

"Admiral, I'm picking up debris ahead, it looks like Jacobs is down. The unidentified vessel is still approaching."

On the video screen the cameras on the small fighter zoomed in to show the faint outline of the damaged, but rapidly approaching transport.

"What do you want to do?" asked Captain Hardy.

Admiral Jarvis looked at the screen but she didn't really have to think too hard. The lives of the sailors, marines and soldiers in the Fleet were too much to risk for one vessel that appeared hostile. Without hesitation she spoke directly to the Captain.

"She is hostile. I can't risk it. Destroy her and quickly!"

"Yes, Sir!" replied the Captain as he moved to the weapons officer's console.

Admiral Jarvis continued speaking with the pilot of the fighter. "Get out of there, she's hostile. I repeat. She is an enemy combatant!" The pilot responded with a simple acknowledgement.

"Permission to fire, Sir?" asked the Lieutenant.

"Do it!" ordered Captain Hardy as he watched the view screen.

It seemed like an age as the weapon system activated. All around the ship were small weapon mounts, each fitted with medium power railguns and rapid-fire projectile weapons. Against a target as small as the transport, the aircraft carrier would have to make use of the point defence turrets. Each one had a maximum range of twenty kilometres, but could launch a devastating barrage of explosive shells that could hold off scores of missiles or attacking fighters.

"She's in range, opening fire!" The Lieutenant hit the automatic defence system.

Lights started to flash along the console as the weapon systems took turns to lock and fire at the ship. First one, then forty separate turrets fired bursts of shot at the craft. From their position on the ship they could see the grey trails from the shells as they blasted out into space and towards the unseen target. The defensive fire stopped almost as soon as it had started. In the distance a tiny yellow flash indicated the weapons had hit something.

"Report!" called out the Admiral.

"Target is off the board, we're clear, Sir," said Captain Hardy.

The officers breathed a sigh of relief. Another attempt to break the blockade had failed, though at the loss of a good pilot.

"General Rivers, you are clear to continue ground operations."

"Aye, aye, Admiral."

Admiral Jarvis took a few steps back and sunk into her chair. With the ground operation still ongoing and the frequent attempts to get near her ships, it felt as if everyone was aiming to make her life as difficult as possible. She could only hope that the arrival of the Army would give the forces on Avagana a chance to recover lost ground and push out the rebels once and for all.

* * *

Spartan watched the black shapes emerge from the clouds. According to his tactical display the approaching vessels were the heavy Landers of the Army. Around these massive vessels were dozens of the small Lightning MKII fighters. A few seconds after the first emerged the dark shapes of more Landers appeared behind them. The roar from their engines took a short time to reach the ground but when it did it was mighty.

"Where are they going?" asked Marcus.

Spartan checked his tactical map, there were no details for the Army units anywhere near his position. He clicked a button to contact Lieutenant Daniels.

"Sir, are the Army units deploying in this area?"

"Negative, Sergeant. I've just been in touch with Captain Mathews, he is further down the line and establishing a high bandwidth link with the Fleet. Apparently the Army units are being landed outside of the cities to start sweeping actions against the enemy."

Spartan zoomed out on his map until he could see some of the others settlements still occupied by Confed units.

"So what about us, Sir? Any reinforcements coming our way?"

"Our orders are to maintain the perimeter and the city defences until relieved by the Army. For now the marine units are to operate as a defensive bastion."

Spartan wasn't impressed. Everything he had learnt and been taught during basic training had shown him that the marines were flexible and well-equipped units designed for movement and rapidity. He couldn't understand why the slow moving behemoth that was the Army, was to be given the job of field combat operations, when the more flexible marines were stuck in the rubble defending the cities. To him it seemed to be a complete role reversal.

Another noise indicated yet more Landers as they roared off into the distance. Smoke trails snaked up from the ground towards one of the massive vessels as two shoulder-mounted missiles rushed towards the hot engines of the Landers. Spartan cringed at the thought of the hundreds of soldiers plummeting to their deaths with the loss of such a major vessel. He needn't have worried though as a wing of Marine Corps electronic warfare jets whistled past and engaged the missiles with their point defence weapons. At the same time the Lander emptied over a hundred ultra hot flares that scattered around the craft to distract the missiles. The fire from the fighters was rapid and accurate. With two brief explosions the threat was neutralised and the Lander was able to continue its journey in safety.

Marcus climbed up the rubble to Spartan's side to get a better view. The difference in mass between them was considerable with Spartan looking far more bulky in the armour. Checking the open plane was secure, Marcus turned back to Spartan.

"How is Teresa doing?"

"Teresa, yeah, well it was going well. But since the landing on Titan I've only seen her a few times," he said in a low tone.

"What's the story with her? Last time I spoke to her she told me where to go when I asked her about home!" he laughed.

"Yeah, sounds like her. She doesn't talk about her home much. I know she hasn't been back for a few years. She's travelled the System for work, I think this was her last choice."

"Last choice, I've heard plenty of people saying the same, though some here actually volunteered. Can you believe that?"

Spartan was lost in his thoughts, thinking back to his time on Prometheus where he had worked as an illegal pit fighter on the many stations in the System. His debts had since been wiped due to him joining the Marine Corps, but that didn't remove the memories of the many fights he'd had. He liked the fighting but not the people involved. It was laced with gambling, prostitution and drugs. He had managed to avoid the worst of it but there were memories he would like to forget, things he never wanted to remember.

"Never believe what?" Spartan asked, completely forgetting or mishearing most of what Marcus had said.

"Forget it. I think we've got more important things to think about. Look!" he pointed out to the horizon.

In the far distance a dust storm was gathering and making its way to New Carlos. Spartan looked around his position, checking on those nearby and the combat units who were starting to relax.

"To your posts, incoming!" he shouted.

The voice commands were instantly transmitted to each of the CES units and speakers fixed to the exterior of the suit sent the audio to everybody within a hundred metres. Nearby he could see Lieutenant Daniels on top of the outer wall checking the approaching storm.

"Sir, any intel on this?"

"Lieutenant Weathers just reported that two Thunderbolts have been brought down. It looked like someone triggered a series of seismic charges along the front line between us and the landing zones for the Army."

"I don't understand. Why would they do that?"

"No idea, Sergeant, if you ask me I reckon they're trying to create cover for an attack on the Army or us, maybe even both. One thing I do know, that dust storm is coming our way and when it hits it will hit fast. Satellite feeds show it will be here in the next three minutes. I suggest we all get undercover, fast!"

"What about the perimeter lines? If we all take shelter we'll leave the line open."

"Shit, you're right. Get the civilians and militia into cover. All armoured units on the front line. Try and keep your heads down and ride the storm. Let's just hope the Zealots don't get through our lines!" The approaching storm started to drown out his voice.

Spartan shouted at the marines, commandos and civilians, doing his best to clear them from the open ground and trenches into areas with cover from the elements. Small groups of marines in their PDS suits ran to the outer line and replaced some of the militia units who had been taking their turn there. A few CES units fired up their power units and stomped forward into their pre-prepared pits for possible battle. In the distance the other companies of marines and civilians did the same.

Marcus, Davis and Humphreys, all men from his own company, lay down along the rear of the rubble wall and watched the storm through the scopes on their L48 rifles. Spartan moved up ten metres behind them locking his armoured legs into position, ready and braced for the storm. To his right a group of a dozen marines rushed forward to occupy another section of the wall. From where he stood he could see two companies of marines covered a wide front.

"This storm had better be over fast or this battle will be finished before it starts!" he said to himself.

The swirling dust and debris was now only a hundred metres from the outer wall and the noise was already as loud as the battle they had fought when first landing at the outskirts of the city.

"Here is comes! Brace yourselves and watch for..." Captain Mathews' voice was cut off as the swirling dust and dirt became a thick fog.

A man tumbled past as Spartan covered his face and fell over backwards. The winds caught his suit but the mass and weight of the armour kept him secure but he didn't feel completely safe. His right leg slid back a few centimetres so he pushed it down harder into the ground. He turned back just in time to see the ground around him disappear as he collapsed thirty metres underground, buried under masses of dust and rock.

"Shit!" he shouted as his visor was covered in rocks.

He had just enough time to hit the seal button, which brought a thick metal shutter down over the visor to protect the vulnerable hardened glass. As it dropped down the visibility in the suit vanished until the internal lights kicked in to illuminate the interior of the helmet. He tried to move his arms and legs but all four were locked into place.

For a second he started to panic then he remembered his training, his people knew where he was and the suit was easily capable of staying secure and sealed for hours of use. At least, he hoped so he thought worringly to himself.

CHAPTER FIVE

The needs for aircraft of all sorts never diminished, even after mankind spread through the worlds of the new Confederacy. These machines comprised transports, strike craft and fighters and all were optimised for operations in a variety of atmospheric conditions. The Marine Corps and Navy concentrated on multi-role variants of common designs, the Army on their specific roles of ground attack and transportation. Unlike the craft used by the Navy, all Army combat aircraft were for atmospheric flight only, with even their versions of the Thunderbolt fighter being fitted with greater weapon loads and tracking pods at the expense of the ability to fight in space.

Aircraft of the Confederate Armed Forces

The CiC was dark and the temperature slightly cool. Unlike most of the sections of the ship it was quieter, just the sound of low voices and tapping on computer displays. The limited illumination came from the subdued tones of the red tube lights fitted along the walls. The computers and display screens gave off multiple colours that flickered around the room, casting hard shadows on the faces of the operators. This was the beating heart of the battlegroup, and from this one room many ships, fighters and ground-based units were coordinated with skill and precision. In the centre of the room was a three dimensional tactical display that currently displayed the disposition of the ground combat units on Avagana. There were already thousands of marines, commandos and army personnel fighting across the continent as well as small garrisons trapped inside their forts in the other colonies. New Carlos was still under attack but the forces of the Army and their heavy armour were rapidly retaking the open ground around the city. In just seven hours two cities had been relieved and two armoured columns were making their way to relieve New Carlos, over a day ahead of schedule.

The heavy armour of the Army was proving decisive, as were the heavy artillery and overwhelming firepower of the unstoppable battalions of soldiers. They were less flexible than the marines but well equipped for the grinding attritional combat of major field operations. With the newly arrived air support from the Thunderbolt and Lightning fighters the ground war was certainly turning around fast. With the arrival of these news forces General Shears had taken over command of all field Army units on Avagana. He was conducting a pincer movement around the northern and southern approaches to the city. According to his estimates the region would be completely pacified by the end of the day. At this rate the Marine Corps forces could be withdrawn to the transports in orbit and on the ground.

In the CiC, Captain Hardy watched over the Fleet, ever watchful of the potential for danger from either the surface or from new vessels arriving from space. On his display he watched the latest batch of landing craft and transports drop down from orbit. The army transports seemed to be able to disgorge an almost unlimited number of infantry and aircraft. Hardy wondered to himself how things may have gone if the Army had been able to land at the same time as the Marine Corps? Still, the whole point of the Marines was that they were fast, flexible and powerful. If they had relied just on the Army, Avagana would have fallen days before.

He noticed the ship's log on the side of one view screen now listed scores of vessels that had tried to pass through the blockade. Some had tried to head for the surface but most were making a break for open space. This number of civilian traffic was going to be a problem if it kept increasing at this rate, as more and more of the fighters were having to be used to help screen craft attempting to flee the warzone. Though craft heading from Avagana were being watched carefully, it was perfectly legal for vessels to travel to and from the other six colonies, and these were the most worrisome.

The heavy metal door slid open and in walked Admiral Jarvis, flanked by two armed guards. They were both commandos with over a decade's experience in space and ground combat operations. The marines wore full PDS suits and were therefore covered in armour from head to toe. Each man carried an L48 carbine with the small calibre module fitted for use in interstellar operations.

The use of the standard large calibre L48 round would be devastating in the confines of such a vessel in space. These men were the only fully equipped units on the ship. The rest would have to break out weapons from the lockers, if and when an emergency occurred. As they entered the CiC, the two additional guards that protected the sensitive part of the ship stepped aside and saluted. Unlike the two marines accompanying the Admiral, these men wore no armour, only standard issue combat fatigues and pistols. The use of heavier weapons was being strictly controlled due to the possibility of infiltration and hijacking throughout the Fleet.

Admiral Jarvis moved directly past them and to the table where General Rivers was checking the campaign details. Her guards stood close by but not too close as to be obtrusive. News had arrived only a few hours earlier of an attempt to secure the bridge of the CCS Santa Maria. Fortunately, her marine guards had managed to prevent casualties. Since then there was a crackdown on all with links to a number of religious factions and left-wing militant organisations.

Captain Hardy and General Rivers stood to attention as she approached.

"Admiral, you received my message?" asked the General.

"Indeed I did. Army units are pushing back the Zealots and their allies. I don't see the problem."

General Rivers hit a few buttons so that the map pulled backwards and towards the coast. Much of the coastline was rocky and packed with large, almost insurmountable cliffs. Three points were flagged on the display where the coast flattened and led to sheltered coves and beaches. Around these areas were large numbers of the enemy moving to the water. Further inland were the rapidly advancing armies of the Confederacy who were snapping at their heels. The coloured markers also indicated a number of utility aircraft landing near the enemy forces.

"What am I looking at?" she asked.

"These are the retreating troops from the attacks in the South. They have been beaten in open battle and are retreating cross-country to the sea. General Shears has ordered several of the armoured units to pursue them, the remainder are helping with the relief of the outposts and cities," he pointed at the moving icons on the map.

"These aircraft appear to be chartered flights that are taking away the retreating units. Most are small, no more than three of four crew but there are a few larger cargo craft that can move a few hundred at a time," explained the General. "Right now I am more interested in securing the colony."

Admiral Jarvis examined the display. "Well, it does mean they will live for another day but for now the security of Avagana is the most important factor. So far this is all good news, what about their shock troops? Are they falling back too?" she asked impatiently.

"This is one of the problems," he zoomed in closer to the waterline. The view enlarged to show numerous vessels, some as small as rowing boats, others the size of passenger vessels, as they helped people aboard. Some of the larger ones were launching their own aircraft to help bring people away from the shore.

"Who are they?"

"We aren't sure yet but the news feeds are saying some of the relief agencies from New Georgia are helping evacuate refugees and civilians from the fighting. Two of the Churches are also funding ships to help them leave the area."

On one of the screens was a video feed from a Navy reconnaissance jet as it blasted past the beach. The cameras clearly showed the numbers of people making their way to the boats and the large number of infantry on the beach helping them board. The soldiers were not Confederate troops, their uniforms were a grey colour and their craft were common to the militia forces of the Seven Colonies.

"Okay, I see the problem. We have civilian forces, as well as what I am sure will be described as peacekeepers, helping to clear them from the battlefield. You realise this will allow them to regroup to continue the fight in the future? Even so, we can't end this revolt without directly engaging their vessels on the coast or in international waters. Any engagement with forces of the colonies will result in hostilities between us and their combined ground forces." She moved the map across to track the movements of the ships. "I assume a full scale conflict between Avagana and the six colonies is a war we cannot win?"

"Not a chance. At present we are winning, their forces are retreating and we are seeing successes across the continent. If the other six colonies declare open support for the uprising we will face the combined forces of their militaries as well as mobilised militia, the religious orders and whatever shock troopers have survived. That's assuming they don't have more hidden away. Also, I would expect the rest of the colonies in the System would come down on one side or another. The entire sector would be ripped apart by civil war, all of this just so we can stop their beaten forces from retreating," he added tersely.

Admiral Jarvis checked the disposition of the naval

assets on the ground, specifically the marines and the limited number of aircraft they had deployed. She looked back at the map of the planet and the six hostile colonies that seemed to be doing everything possible to cause a rift between them and the Confederation Forces. The more she thought about the situation the more she was convinced the other colonies were trying to provoke a shooting war on the surface.

"So it would be in the interest of the insurgents to provoke us into attacking other colonial forces. They could use this to try and drag us, and the rest of the colonies, into a shooting war. We need to be careful. Once they take the survivors away from Avagana, where are they taking them?"

"Well, our reconnaissance handlers on the ground say the civilians are being taken to lots of different locations, some to New Georgia, others directly to the ports for transfer to liners trying to break the blockade."

Captain Hardy interjected at the mention of the blockade.

"Admiral, in the last hour we have intercepted seventeen transports. Each claim they are carrying refugees from the combat area. We've turned three back but the rest were clear. No unauthorised personnel, no weapons and nobody from the religious orders that we know of."

Admiral Jarvis turned back to the General.

"What about their new pets? Surely their experimental

warriors aren't just queuing up and climbing aboard the boats? Everything I have seen so far suggests they are well motivated, strong and able to fight for much longer than regular units."

"Indeed not. At first we thought they were falling back to the coast, but it seems they aren't heading for the coast at all. It's the Zealots fanatics, foreign fighters and other volunteers who are trying to escape along with a number of civilians. Of course it is often hard to tell the difference between them, it's not like they all wear a blue uniform! Most of the shock troops are making their way back underground and into the many catacombs and tunnels they have been working on. We started to try holding them back, but it's safer all round to let them retreat than trying to destroy a cornered animal. The Air Force has had a field day mopping up as they fall back. A large contingent of them is working their way over ground and underground to the Bone Mill."

Admiral Jarvis moved the map over to the infamous site and examined the aerial shots with interest. It was heavily pockmarked from battle and bombs, over two-dozen armoured vehicles were still belching smoke from recent battle.

"I thought the Bone Mill had already been bombarded? Why bother retreating to a smoking hole in the ground? Wouldn't it be better for them to just expend their forces in a final push on the cities?"

"It has, that doesn't stop them making their way back. I have given orders for them to be pursued back to the site but under no circumstances must we try to stop them. We've given them one clear route out of the battle area and they are taking it," he said as he ran his finger along the display. The map zoomed in to the immediate area around the Bone Mill.

"When their forces are contained we will collapse the site once and for all!"

"Bury them alive, General? What about the connecting tunnels? From what we have seen they have extensive underground tunnel networks that travels miles in each direction. How will you pacify them?"

"I have a squadron of Thunderbolt fighters armed with low yield tactical neutron bombs on standby. Once they are secured at the Bone Mill, the strike will destroy the primary structure and the weapon will kill everything within a twenty kilometre radius."

"So you're going to nuke them. Are you happy with using the nuclear inventory from the Fleet? The nuclear option is always one of last resort. What if the colonies respond in kind? We don't want to start a nuclear exchange," she said in a concerned tone.

"I haven't taken the decision lightly. Under the circumstances I think it is the best and most humane way to resolve the problem. A single strike will eliminate this genetic threat, as well as destroy whatever they have underground that has allowed them to create the creatures to start with. The neutron bombs have a much smaller area of destruction, under a kilometre. The radiation damage is short lived and should clear most of the tunnels with little residual radiation. The only other option is with conventional weapons, that will require a prolonged bombardment and is easily avoided by digging down deeper or taking the more remote tunnels."

A red light started flashing on the communications desk. At the same time a continuous drone started to drown out the sound of conversation in the room. It was a sound that was heard only a few times a month and indicated narrowband data from High Command. The communications officer handed a datapad to Captain Hardy who read it then turned and marched directly to the two senior officers. His face was flushed, whether it was from the stress of the operation or the material he had just read, they couldn't tell.

"Admiral, I have a secure transmission from Fleet Headquarters, it has just finished decoding. I think you will want to see it."

"Of course," she said almost dismissively, "thank you, Captain."

She picked up her datapad and examined the contents of the message. It took only a few seconds to read before she sighed and lowered it to her side. The General looked at her, waiting for some comment on the news. She handed him the datapad but continued to explain the contents anyway.

"The signal is a delayed communication from Fleet HQ at Alpha Centauri. Apparently there has been a violent coup attempt on Terra Nova. Over thirty officers killed along with a number of the Council. The infiltration was by Fleet personnel who are currently being interrogated. The coup was led by separatists from Carthago and it says here that the movement is spreading. Some of the colonies are already debating secession from the Confederacy."

"Good God, I thought we had it bad enough in this System," General Rivers sighed.

"There's more, they are warning that several militant monotheistic groups are planning something major and they think genetic manipulation will play a big part in it. Raids on laboratories on the Confederate Research Stations have shown collusion between some of the top biologists, one of whom has been selling data to a terrorist group."

"We could have used this information weeks ago before this started," said a very irritable Captain Hardy.

General Rivers read down the information on the datapad until he came to the last section of text. "It says all traffic from AC has been halted and any ships en route to Proxima have been turned around. A general quarantine alert for the Proxima System has been put into effect until the crisis is resolved."

"I don't understand, Admiral, why are they blocking us?" the Captain asked.

"It is simple. Until the contamination is halted in the home System, they want to shield us from any fallout. They are assuming of course that nothing will have happened here."

"A fat lot of good that will do us now. We are already facing a potential civil war between the colonies here if we don't resolve the situation quickly. What worries me is how much better or worse are they faring compared to here? If you ask me I think Proxima is taking a hell of a beating right now. We've had hijackings, satellite occupation, capital ship engagement and now a full-scale ground war on Prime. How can it get any worse?"

" You're making a joke I assume, General?" said the Admiral sternly. "As I'm sure you are aware, the situation can always get worse!"

The General looked a little uncomfortable at the rebuking before changing the subject. "How long ago was the message sent?"

"Sixty-two days. Anything could have happened since then, hell the entire System could be overrun with Zealots and in the middle of a full-scale colonial war. We need information and we need it fast!" She turned to her communications officer.

"Lieutenant, check the relay link to Fleet HQ on Terra Nova!"

The officer flicked a few buttons and then scanned the various frequencies used by the communication facilities throughout the stations and ships of the Fleet. At first it appeared everything was normal, then the officer realised something wasn't right. He tried a few more channels but they were all the same. Moving his hand across the screen he added various filters to the data streams but nothing changed the seemingly random nature of the noise. He turned back with a look of surprise on his face.

"Sir, nothing, just static. It's like the signal is being jammed with digital noise. Every single channel is the same, from the main feed down to the wideband data streams. I've tried clearance filters and noise reduction and the system can't find anything."

"So whatever is going on at Terra Nova, Admiral, we can assume they will not be sending us any help?"

"Quite possibly. Either way, General, with no communications, intelligence or supplies we're pretty much on our own."

Admiral Jarvis examined her tactical display as she checked on the status of the systems and ships scattered through the Proxima System. She turned to her communications and tactical officers.

"I want a full update on the readiness of all Confed units in the entire System. I need to know the status of every single ship, transports, supplies, stations and personnel. Make sure you include Army and Auxiliary vessels, include everything!"

General Rivers turned and spoke to one of the armed guards before turning back to the Admiral.

"I'll get my field commanders to gather reports on all our units and outposts."

Admiral Jarvis looked at the display zooming out to view the whole System. Coloured dots indicated friendly vessels, lines and discs showed the various shipping lanes and orbits. A flashing circle showed where the CCS Wasp was located around the planet of Prime. Although many of the vessels were centred on Prime, many more were scattered about the System. She started to count them but gave up once she had reached fifty ships of destroyer class or larger.

Up until now most of the ships in action were being used in ad-hoc formations to conduct limited operations. If this campaign were to go on any longer she would need to establish a number of new fleets and squadrons based on the assets available in the System.

"We're on our own here and we need to start planning for a long campaign," she said quietly to herself as she worked out the optimum placement for the vessels.

* * *

Johnson had been sat at his desk for the last two hours and was having a hard time trying to extract the data from the recovered datapad. Normally he would have handed in the evidence but with the way things were looking right now in Yama, the capital of the colony, he would rather keep it to himself. On one of the video screens to his right he had three feeds running. Two were general aggregate lists of news and reports, the third was a live signal direct from the Parliament Building in the centre of the city. There were always areas of competition between the colonies, but from the rhetoric on the floor of the house he was noticing a trend between the conservative religious parties and those of the ruling liberal coalition. There had already been a failed vote by the opposition to send peacekeepers to Prime to halt the Confed forces in their counteroffensive to clear the colony of Avagana.

Johnson turned back to the datapad and the data he had already extracted onto his computer. At first glance the data cartridges appeared to be blank, but examination under his forensic tools had reveal multiple hidden partitions behind the actual wiped data. It was a clever ruse and would stand up to most examinations. Moving the data to his computer had required him to disable several of his own firewalls but it was a risk worth taking. As he moved some of the data to a secure section of his computer system he heard someone approaching. With a deft flick he moved the data and slid over a virtual folder that contained mugshots over the top. He turned to see Agent Petoskey stood over his shoulder.

"You seen the news?" he asked.

Johnson double-checked his screen before turning to the man.

"Yeah, I've got the live feeds running here," he replied as he pointed to the displays.

"Right, you see what the Confeds have been doing? Just got a report that they are attacking civilians with strike planes. Bastards!"

Johnson could feel the question inside the statement. Petoskey was one of the many nationalistic Kerberons who seemed to hate anything off-world. The only thing worse than the Primes to them was the long arm of the Confederate armed forces getting involved in the business of the Kerberos Intelligence Unit. He had no illusions that as a member of Confed Naval Intelligence, seconded to the local unit, his life would be in serious jeopardy if Petoskey suspected he was anything other than a Kerberon loyalist.

"Yeah, a bloody business. Bet you're glad you're not on the exchange programme with Prime, right?" he laughed.

"You're right there!" replied Petoskey as he turned back and walked along the open plan office.

Johnson glanced again before returning to his computer screen. Luckily the data was hidden but a small icon bobbed up and down along the corner of the screen. He gave a quick glance around the office before tapping it to expand a message from one of his old contacts in the Defence

Department. He didn't waste time with extended niceties, he'd sent his contact a message almost an hour ago saying he needed to call in a favour. This was it. With a twist of his right hand he selected positions of the encoded data and dropped it into an encrypted container and sent it to his contact. A single message popped up telling him to wait. Johnson didn't like this part. The longer it took, the longer there was for somebody to notice what he was up to. Voices came from further inside so he increased the volume on his screens and turned to watch the news from Prime. Along the scrolling ticker it said the video link was from a fishing vessel moored half a kilometre from the shoreline of Avagana. The camera zoomed in to show lines of people in their hundreds waiting to be taken away by small boats. Two strike aircraft blasted past and a cry ran up through the passengers as they ducked to avoid the backwash and possible fire. Nothing happened and the craft simply rushed out along the horizon before disappearing from view.

Beep. A low tone indicated another message had arrived, it was his contact. According to the message it said the data was an agenda for a meeting due to take place on one of the stations along the Rim. Only one person was named.

"Typhon?" said Johnson below his breath, he had heard of this man, though from memory there was little known outside of his almost mythical status.

Johnson brought up a secure terminal screen and checked his security database for all information relating to the man known as Typhon. The first page to be found was related to the most recent mention of the man at a rally on Prime. Supporters of the Church of Echidna had placed a plaque at a bombsite in honour of the man bit it had been removed almost immediately. The name appeared to have been mentioned at several other terrorist sites on the planet where it had been used as a chant.

He scrolled through the information till he reached a file from an informant in one of the state owned mines on Avagana. It said a meeting had been attended by known members of the Crimson Brothers, a left wing radical organisation with links to trade unions throughout the seven colonies of Prime. They had originally been one of the smaller unions but after the riots they had split off and become radicalised. The meeting had been convened to plan an attack on the rail system in the name of Typhon and his holy mission.

"Holy mission?" asked Johnson before realising how loudly he had spoken. He looked around, no one was paying any attention.

He refined his search parameters but could find nothing related to the mission, other than some snippets about the darkness beyond the Rim and something else about preparing for the mission. A series of death threats had been received five months ago to the Trade Ministry from a group purporting to be the Yama Defence League. He pulled up another page that described the group. They were a far-right street protest movement which opposed the spread of the Church of Echidna, Church law and Zealot extremism on Prime and Kerberos.

Johnson leaned back in his chair. It was odd, there seemed to be a good number of groups on Kerberos, some with grievances against the state with others more interested in interfering with each other's business. Prime had become the physical battleground of the troubles but it looked like Kerberos was becoming much the same only in a more clandestine and sinister way.

A message popped up, indicating that the rest of the data had been decrypted. He read it carefully. Most of it made little sense as it contained several quotes from scriptures but one but was of great interest. There was mention of a meeting between the factions, and even more importantly, it stated it would be held by Typhon and his children.

"Holy crap!" exclaimed Johnson as he nearly fell from his chair.

If what he was reading was correct, he had discovered a datapad with information relating to a meeting off-world between the leaders of multiple factions and the quasi-spiritual leader of the revolt, known as Typhon. He grabbed his datapad and hit the options to request a secure feed to his contact on the CCS Crusader. Before his pad would connect to the communication system he had to work through the fractal encryption subroutine, an add-on that was fitted only to the equipment used by members of Naval Intelligence. With the correct code entered it connected to the Naval Intelligence subsystem that was piggybacked onto the primary communication channel from the security headquarters.

"If I'm right this meeting could be between all the major players in the crisis," he said quietly as he waited for the system to connect.

Looking at his screen he dragged the icons of each of the factions, groups and people until he had a small group surrounding Typhon in the middle of the screen. He looked at it thinking how many different people and links there were. This group could hold the key to the war and maybe even a peace in the System. They also contained people at every level of government and society throughout Proxima.

He turned to his left checking the status of his datapad, it was taking longer than expected. He just hoped there weren't any issues with the monitoring of his signal or data traffic. It was still interrogating the servers and checking for a secure channel. As he waited he re-looked at the groups mentioned in the message. It implied many more would be there but their names were in code.

"Who are Typhon's children?" he asked as his datapad connected to the CCS Crusader.

With a flicker the screen changed on the pad as it transformed to a writing surface ready for him to communicate through. Normally he would use visual and audio communication, but with something this sensitive he could not afford to risk himself or the person he was speaking with directly.

* * *

"Sir, message from the surface from an unknown source, it says it is an urgent priority communication," said Lieutenant Nilsson.

"It's okay, let it through," Commander Anderson ordered.

He had been waiting for a signal for some time now and he was beginning to think Admiral Jarvis had been a little too optimistic to expect important information so soon. He checked his datapad and selected the correct codes to establish a secure text link with the intelligence contact on the surface. The icons jumped around and then lined up as the cipher was confirmed. The code for the Admiral's agent was valid and the first piece of information to arrive stunned him. It stated that Typhon, the almost mythical religious figure of many of the religions and cults through the System, would be attending a meeting of major organisations in the next forty-eight hours.

As he read the message it occurred to him that it could

be no coincidence that he had picked up a signal to a site out on the Rim that referred to The One. He remembered reading a report some months ago that linked the term along with two of the most extreme organisations on Kerberos. If this intelligence was correct, this could be the breakthrough they had been waiting for. Maybe the meeting and the signals to the Rim were connected.

"I'll take this in my sea cabin, XO, you have the bridge," he said as he marched out of the room.

As he left he walked the short distance to his sea cabin. It was located close to the bridge so that he could be called from sleep or attending to administration instantly. He opened the door and quickly went inside, closing it firmly to ensure he was alone.

The cabin was sparsely equipped, containing just a bunk, desk, toilet facilities and a computer terminal on the wall. It was an improvement over the accommodation used by most of the crew, but only marginally so. The Captain of the ship also had access to far more civilised quarters at the in-port cabin further aft. When he had the time this area was more lavishly furnished, with a separate bedroom and combination sitting room and office.

He brushed his hand across the computer system and selected the options that would initiate a connection with the Fleet at Prime. As the system went through its connection protocols he poured himself a glass of water. The purification system on the battlecruiser had sustained heavy damage, so like everyone else he had to make do. In the corner of his quarters was a plastic container with four litres of lukewarm water. It wasn't great but it was better than going thirsty. Like most of the vessels in the Fleet, this one was capable of displaying the exterior as though the wall was a window. He could see the dark side of the planet below as well as the glint of light from the orbital shipyards just a few hundred kilometres away. In less than an hour the ship would be docked and the injured crew taken away for treatment. The repair work on the ship could take months, maybe even years.

A tone from the computer display signalled the connection was complete. He moved in front of the screen where the image of Admiral Jarvis awaited him.

"Admiral, I have transmitted a copy of the intelligence received from your contact in Yama. The data indicates a high level meeting between multiple enemy assets in the next two days. I feel there may be a link to the previously intercepted signal with regards to something taking place out on the Rim."

There was a pause as the signal travelled the massive distance. As he waited he checked the intelligence from the previous message. The indicators were all there, a number of high-level delegates, mentions of both the One and Typhon, plus an undisclosed location.

"Commander Anderson, your concerns confirm the analysis conducted by my own team here. There are strong links between Typhon and several pseudonyms that we believe refer to him. This meeting is of great interest to me. We have never been able to infiltrate any of the insurgency cells far enough to obtain top-level intelligence on the command structure of the enemy. Please pass on my orders to our contact at Yama and monitor the situation. I will take care of the operation in the Rim personally. Good work, Commander." The display went black.

The Commander took another sip of water before pouring the rest of it back into the container. There was no sense in wasting such a valuable commodity when the resources of the vessel were so limited. The voice of the XO sounded from his cabin's intercom.

"Commander Anderson, I have the pilot tug requesting permission to lead us into the shipyard."

"I'll be on the bridge shortly, give them permission."

"Sir," came the reply.

Anderson straightened his uniform and opened the door to leave his cabin when his video communication unit started up with an urgent communication. He shut the door and moved back inside to check the message. The video lit up to show the face of the Admiral again.

"Commander Anderson, I have just checked your data and it correlates directly with the intelligence from our other units. I think you know how significant this is to current operations. I need you to finish up your work on the Crusader immediately and arrange to get our contact out of Yama. You need to take the fastest shuttlecraft you have and rendezvous with this ship at the attached co-ordinates. I have already started to assemble a team to join you. I will forward a full briefing pack along with the latest intelligence for you within the hour."

The Commander said nothing as he digested what she had just said. He already had masses of work to do with the Crusader and this sounded like a mission unsuited to his skills.

"I, I don't understand Admiral. The Crusader needs my attention and I fail to see how my knowledge will be of use in a small intelligence operation."

There was a delay as before and he stood patiently, waiting for the details. The mission the Admiral wanted to send him on was hardly suited to a man with his responsibilities. The images of the Admiral continued to move but he knew he was looking at a feed that was transmitted minutes ago.

"Commander, this mission is of the highest priority. The location is out on the Rim and you are the most experienced officer in this sector for that region of space. This isn't a request, I need you in the team immediately!"

He understood immediately what she was saying. The intelligence had pointed to the Rim and with the rest of the data he was obviously going to be continuing the investigation in the murky waters of the Rim. It was some time since he had been there and he was well aware of how dangerous it could be to anybody that was inexperienced.

"Understood, Admiral, I will make preparations to leave immediately."

CHAPTER SIX

Contrary to most people's expectations, the use of close quarter weapons was never anticipated until the uprising was well underway. In the decades since the Great War it had become clear that armour and firepower were the highest priority for the valuable marines and soldiers of the Confederacy. In the confines of spacecraft and the underground caverns around the Bone Mill on Prime, the use of high quality edge and thrusting weapons turned the battle into something that hadn't been seen for hundreds of years. A war, that relied on martial prowess and skill as much as ranged weapons and training.

Edged weapons in the Emergency

Teresa lay in her bunk watching the ships through the virtual window. There were very few marines left on the ship, most had been shipped off and only two companies had stayed back as a reserve. They had already been called out four times and on the last mission she had assisted in what could have been a very ugly one. She had finished writing her section for the after action report, something she was not normally expected to do. On this particular occasion there had been a problem with a diplomatic envoy. It had occurred when the team boarded the civilian liner to find a colonial security unit blocking their access to the rest of the ship. Now technically there was nothing wrong with this as a diplomatic vessel was normally granted full privileges by all Confederation vessels. Due to the heightened security in the crisis however, the Fleet under Admiral Jarvis, had full jurisdiction over any vessels in Confederation Space. Luckily they had been able to force their way inside, but two marines had been slightly injured and it was the violence on a non-military vessel that required her input on the operation.

Teresa looked over at her datapad and the report she had just added her information to. The last section had been written in haste and she was starting to regret the language she had used with regards to the official on the ship. She rolled over to grab the pad and inadvertently hit the send button by mistake.

"Oh…great, just what I need!" she muttered to herself at the rather unfortunate incident.

As she lay there considering the chewing out she could expect when her report arrived, she thought about how

Spartan and the others were doing on Prime. She had not seen him for some time now and the last she heard his unit had been dropped into the heaviest fighting around New Carlos. The news on the battle was that it was going well, but she wouldn't be able to relax until she knew the marines were on their way back to the Santa Cruz. It was weird being alone on what now felt like a ghost ship.

She turned back to her window display and looked out to the planet and spacecraft. One of the newly arrived frigates drifted by and she watched in awe of the mighty ship. Teresa had been reading about the ships, along with lots of other military hardware, during her rest and recuperation aboard the Santa Cruz. From memory she knew it was only a fifth the size of her own craft and was built for combat whereas hers was both a training craft and troop transport. The armour was thick and she could see the multiple layers of thick slabs draped over the more vulnerable parts of the ship. She was far from an expert, but from the reading she had done the armour was a mixture of multiple layers as well as ablative and reactive armour. The frigate was equipped with a number of railguns as were most of the warships in the Fleet. She was also configured with the new, much smaller phalanx weapon systems, a variant of the normal point defence turrets. She understood these turrets could track and hit targets from a railgun with a range of over kilometre. In theory the ship could actually stop kinetic shells before they could hit the armour. Even more importantly, the frigates could provide massed defensive firepower for the larger ships. This was something very new and until the last month had been a very low priority. With the epic battle around Kronus, Admiral Jarvis had pulled in every frigate she could find to help protect the vulnerable transports and capital ships. They had yet to be tried in battle but they were needed none the less.

She shook her head, thinking that she was starting to act like a spaceship spotter, one of those pasty nerds that sat at spaceports taking down the names of ships and their registration numbers to store and check with their friends. She shuddered at the thought, that was not her!

She looked back outside where a number of civilian ships were waiting as security teams checked them before being allowed to the leave the planet's orbit. There was something different going on and the movement caught her attention. As she watched, a military shuttle with a Thunderbolt escort of fighters manoeuvred alongside the hulk of the marine warship. She realised it must be somebody of importance to be coming aboard with such a number of people.

A loud buzz echoed through the cabin as the officer on duty announced the departure in one hour of another boarding party for a civilian liner. As Teresa watched the ships moving past, her video display activated to show an image of Commander Malone, the XO of the Santa Cruz.

"Private Morato?" he asked.

Teresa stumbled out of her bunk and stood up firmly.

"Sir," she muttered as she tried to look a little less haphazard.

"Your presence is required urgently in the briefing room in ten minutes," he said before cutting the feed.

Teresa relaxed for a moment before looking around her bunk for the rest of her clothes. She found her blouse quickly trying to put it on and then pulled on her combat boots. As she dragged on the second boot she stumbled and then reached out, catching the side of the bunk just before she crashed to the floor. She managed to avoid hitting anything major she did knock her datapad off the desk. It crashed to the floor with a sound that suggested something not so good had happened to its internals. She straightened herself up and lifted the unit, noting the scratches and marks down the one side. She turned it around to see three cracks along the screen along with a service error on the front.

"Oh…crap!" she swore as she dumped the unit on the desk and then reached around for the rest of her clothes.

* * *

Spartan stood on his own, his CES suit was smashed to pieces and lay around him. It was odd but somehow he was stood atop a massive building, the tallest structure he could see, perhaps half a kilometre tall. He was so high that there were actually clouds around and below his level. The walls of the building were of smooth granite and marked with the holes, pits and scratches of a structure that was worn from decades of exposure to the elements. He looked up at the series of glowing masts and aerials that looked like the extended lines of the spines on a porcupine. Several microware and narrow band dishes were also fitted that pointed out to the horizon.

Spartan was confused. He had no idea where he was or even how he had reached such a high position. He looked down to see he was wearing the armour he had worn months ago during his time as an illegal pit fighter on Prometheus. The breastplate was of gleaming bronze and his legs were protected in metal greaves. He was the epitome of a classical hero. As he looked he noticed the weapons in his hands. It was bizarre because a few seconds ago he was sure he had empty hands. In his left hand was a large metal shield, it was round and covered in odd runic symbols along its face. In his right hand he carried a mace, a savage looking rod of iron with a flanged head made of even heavier metal and sharp edges.

As he stood on the metallic structure surveying his surroundings he saw a number of the dreaded shock troopers. The horribly mutated and genetically altered monsters were the ultimate warriors. Faster, stronger and able to fight longer than any man, they were the new breed of soldier though their origins and allegiance were still a mystery. The first turned towards Spartan and then with a scream it rushed for him. It leapt forward, moving an incredible distance and was quickly joined by a second. They moved faster and with more power than he had ever seen, as if they could float through the air towards him. He slammed his shield into the first but it was easily twice the size and mass of him. The impact knocked him backwards a full metre yet he was able to maintain his posture with his shield out in front. The creature slammed some kind of crude edged weapon down, hitting like a hammer on the thick shield. Spartan was forced to bring his right hand over to help support the shield as more blows struck down. His front foot slipped and he crashed to the ground. Knowing he would die if he stayed there, he flailed out with his right hand and managed to strike the ankle of one of the warriors. It fell down backwards and in a flash Spartan felt he could win. Rolling to the side he narrowly avoided an attack and then resumed his stance, shield in front and mace held behind him, cocked and ready to swing at the enemy.

"Now you die!" hissed the creature.

Spartan wasn't sure he had heard one of them speak before, but took the opportunity to strike the wounded one that was trying to stand up. As his mace crashed into the thing's head he was covered in blood, the spray plastering his face and body armour. Like a screaming banshee the second jumped through the air and smashed into Spartan's shield. He managed to hold the impact but as he moved back his feet were unable to find purchase on the gravelled surface. Then he felt something strange beneath his right heel. He glanced back to check realising it was the emptiness of nothing. He was on the edge of the tower and just centimetres from a long, painful fall that would result in death.

"Come on!" shouted Spartan but there was something odd about his voice, it was as if the very sound was being sucked from his lungs and left him feeling cold.

The creature pounded away and Spartan was once again forced to protect his body with the heavy shield. Spotting an opening he swung his mace and dealt a savage blow to its shoulder. Sensing victory he pushed his shield up to its head and swung the mace low into its stomach. It impacted with force but before the creature collapsed it managed to stumble forwards. Spartan tried to grab at his attacker but it was too late. He fumbled and then fell. The sick feeling of dropping into a great pit washed over him and he seemed to move faster and faster.

He opened his eyes, still screaming loudly before realising he was asleep or perhaps unconscious. There was something odd and unlike anything he'd felt since being knocked unconscious during his pit fighting on Prometheus. His head was pounding, it felt like a drum was pounding repeatedly next to his ears. His eyes strained at the brightness of the light. It reminded him of the movies he'd seen where prisoners were dragged out in front of their captors and forced to talk by starving them of food or shining bright lights into their faces. He shook his head and looked around but could see nothing other than the bright blurred background. He had completely forgotten where he was and for a moment he panicked. His arms and legs were stuck and he couldn't see anything that resembled the real world. Perhaps he was strapped down, in fact he couldn't even tell if he was vertical or horizontal.

As he tried to move his memories started to flood back. The thoughts of the battle he had been fighting, the numbers of marines and CES units fighting a bloody hand-to-hand battle in the city of New Carlos. He strained his eyes, still the light wouldn't clear. He kept still and thought back to the very last thing he could remember. He'd been waiting for the enemy to attack when the terrible storm hit. Yes, the storm. It had been violent and with the cover provided by the dirt and dust the enemy had tried one last desperate assault. He could remember now, the images of the violent storm that had tossed men and machines aside. Calming down he looked inside his armoured visor, looking for any indicators that could give him a clue as to what was happening. Something shook him and a small amount of dust poured though a crack in the side of the visor.

"Fuck!" he tried to spit the dust out of his mouth.

Another violent shake rattled his armour and suddenly he was blinded by more light as it entered in through the side of the helmet. He tried to raise his arms but, with no working motors and the ground still holding him encased, he couldn't move. He was about to shout when the bright light started to ease back until he could make out dark shapes. Some of them were moving and then it dawned on him. Somebody was digging him out, the question though was, who? He pulled his left arm back inside the suit and reached for the self-destruct system. If it was the Zealots there was no way in hell he was letting them take him prisoner. He flicked the switch and activated the system. All it needed was four taps on the button with the correct timing and the suit would detonate, killing him but hopefully taking a few of them with him. It was a small explosive charge, anything more powerful could cause damage to friendly units or transport ships if there was an accident. It was easily enough to exact a little vengeance however.

"Come on you bastards," he muttered through clenched teeth, "I'm waiting for you."

* * *

Teresa hurried along the corridors of the CCS Santa Cruz as she made her way to the briefing room. She had pulled on her uniform but didn't have the time to sort out her hair or to attempt anything more formal than her basic gear. She just hoped it was something important like a fire rather than a formal occasion. If it were the latter, she would be in big trouble!

As she moved past the files of marines she started to worry that something bad had happened. Maybe it was her family, maybe Spartan? Who knew, all she did know was that the message was unexpected and the waiting was killing her. As she rushed down the walkways a number of marines were forced to jump out of her way, one almost striking his head on a bulkhead before a sergeant pushed out his hand to stop him.

"Hey! Watch your step, Private!" he barked.

Teresa signalled an apology with her hand but kept going at the same speed. The entrance to the briefing room was only a short distance ahead and as she rounded the corner she came to an abrupt halt. At the entrance to the room was a group of four armed marines, each watching both sides of the corridor for signs of trouble. She moved towards them but before she could reach within fifteen metres, one of them turned and closed the distance.

"You Teresa Morato, Private?" he asked.

"Yeah, that's me. What's going on?"

The marine guard held out a scanner for her identity card. With a quick scan he had her details including a detailed colour photo and all her basic statistics. He looked for a few seconds as he satisfied himself that she was who she said she was.

"Just go in," the guard indicated towards the door.

Teresa looked back, concerned at entering a room that was guarded so heavily. As she got nearer she felt a pang of worry as she considered this might be related to the numerous rumours of marines being rounded up with any kind of suspicious past, for security reasons. She needn't have worried though for when she entered the room there were just a handful of people. One of them was Admiral Jarvis, to the right were four marines including Bishop and Kowalski, the two marines she'd already met. To the side of the room was a virtual presence device that allowed a projected image of the faces of two more men. One was a Naval Commander in his service uniform, the other appeared to be wearing plain clothes. The door shut behind her and they all looked at her before the Admiral indicated for her to approach.

"Private, I understand you were wounded during the operation on Kronus? Are you fit for duty?" she asked.

For a moment Teresa considered answering no. She still had some time left before she was supposed to rejoin the combat unit but this group had the look of something different, something unusual and that always got her attention.

"I'm fit and ready for duty, Sir," she said quickly.

Admiral Jarvis smiled as she turned back to the others.

"Good, if you'll come with me to the display, I have something to show you."

The small group moved to the centre of the room where a flat table-based computer had been set up. Above the table was a projected model of the Rim and its thousands of moons, rocks and stations. Admiral Jarvis spoke first.

"As you are no doubt aware, you are all here for a mission of the utmost importance. Each one of you has been selected for a reason deemed necessary for the completion of the mission. When you leave this room you will be taken to an unmarked shuttle that will rendezvous with a vessel that is already on its way to the Rim. I need not tell you that this mission is top secret, you will report directly to me and me alone! "

The Admiral looked at the group of five people, checking their expressions and gauging their commitment to the operation. Satisfied they had understood the gravity of the situation she continued.

"This entire sector is being split apart by a combination of forces, some of which we are only now beginning to discover. The primary insurgency has been from several of the militant religious groups. We are now seeing movement from separatists on some worlds with potential support from corporations on Kerberos. What we don't have is any full idea of their overall plan, and even more importantly, we have no idea which person or group is co-ordinating these actions against the Confederacy. What I can tell you is that this action is a clear and present danger to the peace and stability of our very way of life."

She turned back to the display and the map zooming in to the specific sector of the intelligence collected by the Crusader.

"Somewhere in this area is a meeting of leaders, possibly even those behind the command of this emergency. Your mission will be to locate the source of the gathering and to infiltrate it. In the last hour we have narrowed the area down to three stations and seventy asteroids in Sector 3G. Once you are in range you should be able to narrow your search even more."

Pressing several buttons the map pulled back until finding a tiny dot in the middle of open space. The display zoomed in to show a medium cargo vessel, one of the thousands that trawled the system carrying minerals, supplies and equipment. There was nothing especially interesting about the ship.

"This is the Tamarisk, she is a modified transport that we have equipped as a Q Ship."

"Q Ship?" asked Bishop with a confused look on his face.

"Yes, she is to all intents and purposes a conventional unarmed transport with the usual number of crew and cargo sections. As a Q Ship she has been fitted with concealed weapons, enough to almost match a gunboat in combat, she will be your transport to the Rim. You might wonder why we aren't just sending a number of military vessels into the area, I will let Commander Anderson of the CCS Crusader explain."

On the virtual presence equipment the face of Commander Anderson remained impassive. As they waited Teresa stepped forward so that she was within earshot of Bishop.

"Why did they choose us?" she whispered.

Bishop turned and signalled for her to keep quiet as the voice of Commander Anderson came through the communication unit.

"The Rim is the most dangerous region of space in this entire sector. I have conducted several campaigns in the past there and can confirm that any naval vessels reaching within three hours of the Rim will be detected and reported. If we want to get in quietly for an intelligence gathering operation we will have to make use of conventionally registered commercial vessels. The Tamarisk was damaged in a collision three months ago and has been modified during her repairs. The plan is simple. We will all rendezvous on the Tamarisk in the next twenty-four hours and continue to the Rim where we have arranged to complete a deal with an equipment trader called Antonius from Carthago. That is where you come in, Private Morato," he said as he looked towards her.

"Me?"

"Yes. We have checked your background and you have

the accent, know-how and local knowledge of Carthago to help us get close. We will need you to elicit the trader's trust so that we can gain access to the more sensitive locations in the area," the Admiral answered.

She continued. "You have all been chosen for your exemplary combat and service records. You will travel as the ship's crew and carry only civilian and black market weapons. It is your job to provide escort for the team and firepower if anything goes wrong. Commander Anderson will be in charge of the operation and you will be assisted in your task by Agent Johnson from Naval Intelligence."

She moved the map into a wider view to show the entire sector with the burning star of Proxima Centauri circled by the many planets of the System. Each of the planets and component colonies appeared as various shades of purple, red patches showed where fighting, attacks or trouble had been reported. It was obvious was that Prime was the heart of the current troubles. Kerberos had several patches but it was also obvious it could follow in the same direction of Prime.

"As you can see, the entire System is balanced upon a knife edge and just one more major incident could create a domino effect that we will not be able to manage. Even more important is that we believe there will be no more reinforcements from Alpha Centauri, certainly not for a number of months. This means the only forces at our disposal are those already in the Proxima System."

The room was briefly quiet before the Special Agent joined in.

"I have received additional intelligence that I will share with the team when we meet on the Tamarisk. It is of course imperative that nobody is aware of your mission or where we are going. Admiral, I must make arrangements prior to our rendezvous."

Admiral Jarvis moved directly in front of the camera fitted to the virtual presence device.

"I will speak with you upon your arrival, God speed."

The image on the display flickered and then vanished. The face of the Commander expanded and filled the remaining space.

Admiral Jarvis turned to the group, looking specifically at Teresa.

"A shuttle is already waiting for you. Take the C Deck, it is unmonitored all the way to the craft. Once you reach the Tamarisk and have been briefed by Commander Anderson I will speak to you again. You must take no additional items with you, no clothes, nothing of a personal nature."

The Admiral walked towards the further wall where a number of boxes were stacked. She lifted the lid of the first and pulled out a set of overalls placing them on the table.

"There are clothes and equipment for each of you along with papers and identity chips. Do not leave this room until you have removed everything you are wearing and replaced it with the gear we have selected."

Bishop, Kowalski and the other two marines stepped forward and started checking through the boxes. Each had their own box with everything they could imagine they might need including a spare set of clothes. Teresa joined them and was mortified to see that unlike the marines she had clothing and paraphernalia of a ship's captain. She turned back to the Admiral.

"I, uh, don't understand. Why?"

"It will be clear when you have time to read the full briefing pack waiting for you in the shuttle. Your background in mining and the troubles on Carthago will give you the credibility we need for a rogue trader in this part of the Confederacy."

Teresa raised one eyebrow, obviously a little surprised at the role given to her and also a little apprehensive at the responsibility she had been granted. She turned back to the box and with a tug pulled her green vest off to put on the clothes left out for her.

A hand tapped her on the shoulder, it was Bishop who was staring at the partially clad woman. The look on his face was a mixture of amusement and also a serious reminder about the mission.

"I think you need to change everything," he said with a wink.

Teresa looked down, realising she was wearing her issue sports bra. Like most of their gear it was a faded grey colour, much like the colour the armour and equipment of the Marine Corps was painted in. She turned her head in annoyance and then in one quick movement pulled the bra above her head. Bishop looked a little surprised and perhaps uncomfortable as he turned back to his own box.

Teresa smiled to herself, finding the whole situation rather amusing. That was until she examined the rest of the clothing, it was less than perfect.

* * *

The light started to fade and Spartan was finally able to see through a few gaps in the dust covered visor. He could make out shapes moving about and could only guess they were people. But which ones he had no idea.

"Spartan?" somebody shouted.

He strained to hear as he tried to make out the sounds. The grinding and hammering of machinery came from all around him. Then he felt dizzy, before a jarring impact made him realise he had just fallen down. He shook his head and prepared to hit the button to trigger the internal charges.

"Spartan, it's Marcus. Are you okay?" came the voice again.

Spartan eased back on the controls, it looked like he might be alright after all. He tried to peer through the visor but he was evidently on his back and looking up at the sky. The sound of electric motors and a buzzing from his right arm confused him.

"We're opening up the suit, hang in there, buddy!"

The buzzing sound continued until with a clunk the armour around the inside of his right arm popped open to reveal his skin to the cool air of Prime. More whines and clunks came from around the suit as the damaged sections were removed. The torso section pulled open in two parts and helping hands pulled him out of his suit and into the open air. Already his eyes were becoming accustomed to the light. The nearest was a marine, he could tell by the distinctive shape of the PDS suit.

"Holy shit, Sarge, we thought we'd lost you in the middle of the storm!" he said with obvious relief.

Spartan shook his head and looked around, getting his bearings. He was almost exactly where he had been standing when the storm him. Around the area a number of the shock troopers' bodies were being dragged away, while other vehicles were helping to clear the rubble and masonry from the storm and battle.

"What happened? Did we win?"

Marcus moved up closer to Spartan, placing his hand on his shoulder to help stabilise him.

"Better than that, the storm was their last attempt to break the siege. We broke them on the walls and their survivors tried to escape across the plains," he said before being interrupted by another marine.

"Escape? You kidding me, the Air Force has been bombing the crap out of the area for the last hour. Nobody is getting out of there alive," he said with undisguised glee before turning back and continuing his work.

Spartan's eyes were now back to normal and as he looked about the scene of the battle, he was amazed at the carnage and death. Bodies from both sides were stacked up as well as abandoned equipment and weapons.

"How is our CES platoon, Marcus?"

"Not great, I think only a couple of the units are still working, I'll tell you what though. If it hadn't been for them we would have broken. No way could we have held off the attack in that storm. I saw some of your guys taking on two or three of those troopers and come out on top," he beamed at Spartan.

He turned back to see his damaged and scorched armour on the ground. There were multiple holes in the framing and some of the panels were torn from falling debris and projectile fire. He bent down and examined the visor with its many scratches and holes.

"You were lucky, if it wasn't for that suit you would have been crushed like the three marines that were dragged down with you."

A trio of Thunderbolt fighters blasted overhead, each one leaving a supersonic shockwave in their wake. Spartan could see the fuel tanks and extra missiles slung under their wings and they moved off to continue harassing the retreating forces.

A small group approached from the left, it was marines and civilians as well as an army officer. They were moving slowly down the line speaking to the officers and NCOs as they went. Spartan recognised Lieutenant Daniels in the middle. Like Spartan he was no longer wearing his CES suit and had reverted to the standard issue PDS. As Spartan watched them the officer noticed him and, after saying a few words to those around him, made directly for him. As he came nearer Spartan noticed he wore a bandage around his right shoulder.

"Sergeant, damned pleased to see you made it!"

He lifted his arm to salute but was stopped by a spasm of pain that sent pangs through his body.

"Sir, what happened to your shoulder?"

"Oh, yeah, my war wound!" he laughed. "In the middle of the storm part of the apartment block behind us collapsed. Some of the masonry hit our machine gun post and I took a fragment on my suit. It bloody well hurt too! I'll tell you what, without the suit I'd be a dead man. I owe you that one."

A man holding a satellite radio ran over to him. "Sir, I've got Captain Mathews for you."

Lieutenant Daniels signalled to Spartan that he needed a moment before turning to the man and the radio. As he started a long conversation with the Captain, Spartan turned back to Marcus and two more marines who'd wandered over.

"Holy shit, you should have seen the hole that took you. Man, that was some crazy business," said the first.

The second was pointing to a massive breach in the outer barricades.

"Just after you vanished a dozen guys came through that hole. We don't know what they used but it blasted a hole five metres wide."

"How did you stop them?" he asked, genuinely interested in hearing their stories.

"Well, a mix of guts, stupidity and luck! One of them had thrown a demolition charge up into our position. James here, our illustrious private, managed to grab it and tried to throw it back from his position on the OP. When he threw it the pack got stuck on the framing out there," Marcus said as he pointed to an open space with a crater in the ground. "Luckily for us, it exploded as they came up from the breach and brought down half the structure on their heads."

"You lucky son of a bitch!" said Spartan, now laughing at the story.

"Hey, Sergeant!" shouted Daniels from a few metres away. "You're not going to believe this!"

"What do you mean, Sir?"

"We've just received word from Kerberos that a Summit has been called between the colonies of Proxima as well as with representatives from the militant organisations."

"So?" asked Spartan who looked nonplussed.

"So?" responded Lieutenant Daniels. "The Zealot leadership has announced an immediate ceasefire while the summit takes place."

"Ceasefire? Here, on Prime?" Marcus asked surprised.

"Yes, as of fifteen minutes ago all fighting on Prime has stopped. Peacekeeping forces from the other six colonies here are still taking away any survivors from the insurgents. We have orders to let them leave, right now we need to consolidate our hold here."

"Am I getting this right?" asked James. "The war is over?"

"Not the war, but for now we have a break. I have orders from Captain Mathews to collect all our people and equipment for extraction in sixty minutes. Looks like we're going home to the Cruz!"

"Back to the Cruz?" asked a surprised Spartan.

"Indeed," Lieutenant Daniels replied with a wry smile.

Spartan looked around him, at the equipment and fires that were still burning. There didn't seem to be much of a city left but he knew they had done well. All he could hope for now was a break from the fighting. Even a few days would be nice.

"Hey, brother, I know what you're thinking!" said Marcus as he slapped his hand down onto Spartan's arm. "Santa Cruz here we come!"

CHAPTER SEVEN

Two years before the outbreak of the Great War a religious controversy erupted through the colonies of mankind. The argument started with a simple schism of the Church of Man, the largest of the cults on Terra Nova. The problem was the display of icons and their use. Until the schism it was normal practice for icons to only be kept in the churches. When the Bishop of the City of Echidna declared icons could be carried by anyone the schism was formed. His martyrdom saw the birth of the new religion and the first of the religious conflicts.

The Iconoclast Controversy

The journey to rendezvous with the Tamarisk had been slightly shorter than expected. Even so, twenty hours in a cramped shuttle with the four marines had been a trial in itself and Teresa needed some space to move. As they reached within ten kilometres of the ship, the display at the front of the shuttle changed from the automated navigation page to a video communication relay with Commander Anderson who was already onboard.

"Greetings, I hope your journey was uneventful."

The video showed the officer but from his surroundings the ship looked less than spacious. Commander Anderson was actually stooping under a bulkhead so that he could see the screen. It didn't inspire confidence in Teresa and her hope for more space to move around in. From the port window she could see the ship getting closer. The engines of the vessel were on full burn as the transport propelled towards the Rim and their destination. Only a fast craft like their shuttle had a chance of meeting them in time without slowing down the Tamarisk and risking the mission.

"Agent Johnson is already onboard and I have taken delivery of items of equipment that should prove useful to our mission. That is all for now, we will discuss this in more detail upon your arrival. Please watch the gravity when you come aboard, due to the acceleration we are operating at a few percentage points over normal. Anderson, out," he said and the screen cut to black.

"Short and sweet," said Kowalski.

"Just like Teresa!" laughed Bishop.

Teresa turned to the two of them and gave them a look

that stopped their amusement in their tracks.

From inside the shuttle the Tamarisk was definitely less than inspiring. She was an old ship by any standards and though she had been well repaired, no effort had been made to beautify the vessel in any way. The outer hull was pockmarked with scratches and marks from her many voyages. The shape was unusual, as the vessel looked like three spheres joined together by a series of gantries running along the outer parts of the ship. As they moved ahead she could see that the spheres were just the last third of the ship. The remaining middle of the ship consisted of a dozen rectangular sections designed for carrying mechanical parts and supplies. Only the front of the vessel appeared remotely friendly, with its rounded nose and many windows installed for the crew and passengers. From the datasheets Teresa had been reading on the way, she knew the ship could carry up to thirty passengers at a time. It contained enough sleeping room and storage for this number for up to six months.

"No rotating sections? I take it the ship is a zero-g environment craft then?" Teresa asked as she leaned over to Kowalski and Bishop who were sitting in front of her.

"You've never been on a clipper before?" asked a surprised Kowalski.

"No, why would I?"

"True. Still, clippers work like any of the high-speed ships that we use to move people and materials through the System. They're just the same as the colony ships and military transports."

"I don't understand, same in what way?"

Kowalski looked at the other marines with a look that told Teresa it was a question you shouldn't need to ask.

Private Williams, the youngest of the group and an avid reader of anything technical or military, turned around in his seat so he could see Teresa. He looked at her for a moment before receiving a withering stare. He looked nervous, something Teresa found amusing for a marine.

"Uh, the high speed ships are all designed to be able to move their cargos quickly through the System. This is usually used for volatile or time critical items, sometimes even the military use it for the rapid transfer of troops to a warzone. It is expensive and not all the ships are equipped to travel in this way."

"Explain it to me, please?" she said in a tone that Bishop and Kowalski instantly recognised as the dry sarcasm she used with them. Williams hadn't noticed though and launched into a simplified description.

"If you want to travel between two places in the Confederacy you will need speed, a lot of it or it could take you months or years depending on your destination. Many ships will just accelerate to a certain speed and then coast using Ion thrusters to maintain a speed to their destination. That is how most of the heavy transports work. In fact some never technically slow down, they follow a continuous path on their elliptical courses through Proxima. They have to be loaded and unloaded at speed by other craft."

"Yeah, and what about the high speed ships?"

"Oh, right. Well, to go farther these ships spend all of their time accelerating. So they leave and fire their engines and keep them on till they reach the halfway point. Then they rotate around and fire the engines in reverse and continue for the other half."

"Ah, that's why we have gravity in this shuttle?" asked Teresa.

"Uh, yeah, you only just worked that out?" Bishop laughed.

Barca, the fourth marine in the group leaned into the conversation.

"I've always wondered about that actually. Most of our ships have rotating sections to provide artificial gravity for long journeys. What happens with the high-speed ships? Surely constant acceleration will create a g force that will effectively create an amount of gravity."

"Holy crap, you actually studied?" laughed Williams.

"You're a funny guy, Williams," responded Barca.

"Well, that is why the ships tend to used a linear, fixed acceleration. For ships carrying crew it is normal to stay on a 1g burn. So the ship maintains a continuous level of acceleration that is approximately 1g in thrust. Providing the ships are designed for the trips the rear of any inhabited sections will become the floor. You might have noticed the signing on the marine transports that implies you could walk in multiple places depending on the orientation of the ship. If the vessel is coasting or moving at low levels of acceleration we use the rotating sections. Once the ships speed up the rotating sections can be stopped and the gravity is provided by the thrust alone."

"Interesting. We didn't do that on the Santa Maria when we made our way to Prime," said Teresa.

"That doesn't surprise me, the Maria is also used as a training ship. You will have spent most of the journey coasting while picking up new recruits and supplies. You signed up in Prometheus as well, right?" he asked.

Teresa nodded.

"Well, it is very dangerous to use the high speed transport option in an area like Prometheus. Hell, I know a few decades ago an army transport tried a direct run to the planet and was lost with all hands in the storms. I think a few thousand died in that incident."

"Look, we're nearly there," said Bishop.

The marines watched the vessel, the computer handling the entire operation as the shuttlecraft approached the side of the ship. The process appeared painfully slow but the marines knew that both craft had been accelerating until this point and at incredibly high speeds. With a sickening feeling in their stomachs the primary engines of the shuttle cut off in synchronisation with the Tamarisk. At first the larger ship appeared to drift ahead but minute adjustments by the shuttle's computer helped them maintain the speed.

"Crap, weightless again," Bishop moaned.

With the two spacecraft now travelling at a constant speed the shuttlecraft moved sideways, the small manoeuvring jets helping to nudge the craft inside.

"Uh, are they going to let us in?" asked Kowalski.

As if on cue a large metal shutter raised to reveal a cramped hangar space. Teresa noticed two more craft already stowed inside. One looked like a civilian shuttle, similar to the one they were in but far older and undoubtedly much cheaper. Clamped next to the shuttle was what looked like a Marauder a larger version of the Thunderbolt fighter that could carry extra crew. She turned to Bishop.

"Is that what I think it is?"

"You bet your ass it is. I never thought I'd see one, the Marauder is pretty rare these days. Most have been scrapped or converted back to Thunderbolts. I guess they think we might need something with a pit of a punch."

Their shuttle moved slowly inside the hangar space and alongside the other craft. No sooner were they past the shutters, they started to close again. The blackness of the hangar was lit by the interior lights of their shuttle alone. Teresa sat quietly, waiting for their automated docking to complete. Their craft rotated a full ninety degrees before approaching one of the landing clamps to the rear of the space. With a final clunk the shuttle shook and a series of green lights flashed around the airlock and various displays on the walls. Teresa made to move before Bishop's hand held her shoulder.

"No, not yet, we are still coasting. Wait till we get the double green before getting up."

Teresa looked at him, a little confused as to what was going on. Then a shudder shook through the shuttle and she could feel herself being pushed back into her seat. She felt heavier and heavier until finally they must have been back to normal gravity. A hiss echoed through the passenger area as the airlock opened to a small doorway leading into the hangar. Releasing her harness Teresa expected to float out, completely forgetting the entire point of what had just happened and instead found she was pinned in her seat. She looked over at the amused face of Williams.

"The acceleration, remember?" he laughed.

Teresa stood up and walked to the doorway, her legs aching from sitting for so long. As she passed through the airlock she reached the open space of the hangar and looked around inside the darkened area. Bishop was out next, quickly followed by the others as they yawned and stretched.

"Well, we're here," said Kowalski.

A noise came from the far wall, followed shortly by a metal hatch opening up. A dull yellow light poured in and hurt their eyes for a few seconds as they adjusted to the brightness. Through the light stepped two men, both in civilian clothes. The scrawny man at the front Teresa recognised as Commander Anderson. She straightened up and saluted, the other marines quickly followed.

"Welcome to the Tamarisk," said the Commander. "Before we get started you need to get rid of that habit. As of from now you are a civilian crew on a civilian ship. Until our mission is completed there will be no saluting, mentioning of rank or following of naval protocol. Understood?"

"Sir!" came the unanimous reply.

Commander Anderson just stood there. He said nothing before turning to the stranger to his right. The man was dressed in civilian clothing and wore a light waistcoat that was marked and scruffy.

"This is Johnson, from Kerberos."

"You're the Special Agent Admiral Jarvis spoke of?" asked Teresa.

"Not today, just called me Johnson."

Teresa nodded, the changed protocol on the ship finally starting to sink in.

"Follow me," said the Commander as he turned and walked back through the doorway. Johnson followed immediately behind. Teresa looked back at the other four marines who smiled nervously, then turned and went through the doorway and into the ship.

* * *

Lieutenant Daniels was first off the assault shuttle. He turned and shook Spartan's hand before stepping down to the hangar floor.

"Good work again, Sergeant, we'll meet for a full debriefing in an hour," he disappeared along with the scores of other people piling out of the other craft.

Spartan was next off and as his feet hit the cold metal he felt a pang of relief to be back aboard the old ship. Several of the craft had already arrived prior to them with the wounded and urgent passengers, which Spartan noted there were many. He stepped to one side and counted in the men from his platoon as they moved in slowly, there were only nineteen. Roughly half of the unit was dead or wounded. Thankfully he noted that the bruised, but implacable Marcus, strolled out and shook his hand.

"Spartan, thought I'd lost you on the way up," he said happily.

Several marines were carried past on stretchers before Spartan spoke.

"I spoke to Lieutenant Daniels on the extraction. He said the Santa Cruz is joining the rest of the marine units at Kerberos for reinforcement and medical attention."

"Kerberos? What about the fight on Prime? We can't just leave the colony."

"True, but garrison duty and engineering is the job of

the ground pounders. Right now we are in no shape for continued combat operations. Have you seen the casualty reports? By all accounts our units should be pulled out of the line for six months or more."

Tex and Travis, two of the marines that he had spent some time with on Prime, climbed out and joined the little group. Tex was starting to warm to Spartan, though Travis as usual was still quiet. The day before they had landed on Prime, Spartan had been training with the two of them. Being a new arrival to the commandos he hadn't fitted in very well. It wasn't helped by the fact that some thought he'd had a lucky break in the fighting on Kronus, seeing as they all had long and distinguished careers in the Marine Corps prior to selection for their elite unit.

"Spartan, that was some crazy ass shit going on down there!" laughed Tex.

Spartan looked at him and smiled. Even in all this blood and trouble he was glad to see the entire ship no longer viewed him as a lucky break. He had proven he had the skill and the drive to be worthy of the commandos. He suspected with the casualties they had sustained and the growing problems throughout the System that his skills would be needed very soon.

"When you're done I want to see you in the mess, we have things to discuss!" he said before the two men left the hangar.

James O'Reilly was the last man out and Spartan

recognised him from the action prior to the storm. As he walked past, Spartan tapped him on the shoulder. The marine looked startled and stared into his eyes before moving on, ignoring everyone.

"That's not good."

"Yeah, you can say that again, Marcus, I need to speak with Daniels, we've got a few marines here that need some attention. We got hit bloody hard down there, much harder than we should have. I'd really like to know what the hell is going on. Why is there this revolt and who is behind it? No way are those shock troopers a small experiment, they had thousands of them," said Spartan, his brow tightening.

"I know what you mean. Some of the guys back on the surface reckon it is some kind of a feud between some of the groups that first came out here. Personally I think that's a crock of shit. Somebody has something to gain out of this, I bet the Zealots, the troopers and the rest of them are all somebody else's pawns."

The two left the space in the hangar and made for the airlock that led into the main walkways of the Santa Cruz. As they walked through the large airlock it automatically sealed behind them. It was immediately obvious that things were not looking good. There was a lot of blood on the floor and marine medics were running back and forth as they carried blood packs and supplies.

"Shit, this is bad!" said Marcus.

"Yeah, like I said, this isn't some simple religious revolt.

We've got a much bigger problem on our hands," muttered Spartan.

"Well, no way are we going back into action like this. When can we expect to be reinforced?"

"Who knows? From what I've seen they keep sending us in. Maybe somebody will take a look at the figures and realise we aren't immortal."

"Speak for yourself," laughed Marcus, "Come on, I don't know about you but I need a drink."

They walked on past the first airlocks and bulkhead doors that led to the sickbay and recreation area. Marcus started to talk before noticing he was on his own. Turning around he saw Spartan reading a message on his datapad.

"What is it?"

Spartan said nothing for a short while longer as he continued reading whatever it was that he was looking at. Marcus became more concerned when he noticed Spartan's face tense up. He'd already seen that down on the scarred battlefield of New Carlos. Spartan looked up from the pad.

"It's from Captain Mathews, he wants to see me about Teresa," he said slowly.

"Teresa? I thought she was still recuperating from her injuries?"

"Yeah, so did I." Spartan looked about, getting his bearings.

"Hey, where is he?"

"He wants to meet me in his quarters, Marcus, alone."

The two stood for a moment before Spartan made to move. Marcus grabbed his arm before he could leave.

"Listen, I'll be waiting in the rec room. You come and see me right away, understood?" he said firmly.

Spartan nodded, saying nothing before rushing off down the corridor.

* * *

General Rivers surveyed the tactical display of Prime in great detail. No matter how the battle was going he always seemed to be at the map, watching the minute detail of the action and contacting the field commanders at regular intervals. As he stood there he looked worried, as though he was waiting for something terrible to happen. He turned around to face the video-link with General Shears on the surface below.

"General Rivers, I understand your concerns. I can confirm that my local forces have now fully secured the colony. As we speak, we are assisting with rebuilding efforts on the main highways and transport links. New Carlos will be back in business in less than six months," he said dismissively.

"I am well aware of the tactical situation. You have still not answered my questions. Why have you sent all marine forces away from Avagana? The commandos needed to come back of course, they are for specific operations but our other units and specifically the 12th Regiment, have been playing a critical part of defending the colony. Are you sure that Colonial and Confederate Army units are sufficiently equipped and positioned to defend Avagana against any possible attempts to attack it?"

"Of course, and I cannot fail to see the implication that your precious marines are more valuable and more important to the defence of Prime. We of course appreciate the efforts and sacrifices of all Confederate Military forces, including the Navy, Marine Corps and the Army. With the peace talks on going, and no hostile forces in the colony, I see no reason why the marines need to stay here. We still have support from the Army, and I am happy to continue assisting with their use and deployment on Prime. We are better equipped to conduct long term operations here than you are, if we need help we'll be in touch," he then signed off.

The entire room was silent. Those who heard the conversation were keeping their heads down, the rest carried on as though none of them had seen anything happening. Nothing could hide the fact that General Rivers was furious. He slammed his fist down onto the table in a rage that grabbed the attention of every crewmember in the CiC.

"That arrogant son of a bitch!" he roared.

Almost simultaneously with his outburst the door to

the CiC opened and in walked Admiral Jarvis and her ever-watchful bodyguard.

"General, I see you and our friends on the surface have come to an understanding?" she said with a wicked smile.

The General looked as though he had something to say and then did his best to curb his voice. It was one thing to lose his temper when shouting at the table, quite another to lose his temper in front of the Admiral.

"Something like that. It would appear General Shears is convinced he can maintain and defend Avagana unassisted by the Marine Corps. I am concerned that he is trying to politicise the situation rather than ensuring the region is cleared and kept cleared."

"I understand exactly, General. Even so, I think it might not be a bad thing for us to regroup away from, what I'm sure you will agree, is a meat grinder of an operation. Confederate Forces are spread thin throughout Proxima and with no sign of reinforcements, I am inclined to try and maintain a flexible reserve in case of any more emergencies. After all, only the marines and the Fleet can respond quickly and strongly in a short period of time. Let General Shears have his moment in the sun, for now we have the big picture to concentrate on and there are a few things that will have to change."

"Change?" asked the General.

"With us having no contact with Alpha Centauri our chain of command stops in this room. All military forces in this sector need to be assembled and more importantly, an understanding must be reached between the civilian governments of the colonies and our forces. We must work together. It is not a case of us versus them. If we are not careful we could end up doing the job of internal policing, and if that happens we will soon become the enemy rather than the friend of our citizens."

General Rivers considered her comments for a few seconds. He understood how the military could be transformed from friend to enemy in a matter of days. He also had an uncomfortable feeling in his stomach that they were damned either way. They could use a heavier hand to protect citizens or they could step back now that a ceasefire had been declared and hope that hostilities wouldn't recommence.

"I agree with your assessment, Admiral, though I have my reservations about the intentions of the politicians on both Prime and Kerberos. These uprising have substantial technological and financial support. This cannot be coming from grassroots terrorist support mechanisms. I suspect those behind the troubles are much higher up than that."

He paused as he considered what he had just said, some of which had only just occurred to him. If there was someone, or at least a group behind the troubles, what would they have to gain? Why would they have pulled strings for a ceasefire? He could only assume they needed time to rebuild before attempting further uprisings and coups. He looked back to Admiral Jarvis.

"What are you proposing?"

"Well, as you know the marines have been sent to Kerberos for a period of rebuilding and re-equipping. They are also being sent there so that we can make a statement as the peace talks are ongoing."

"Yes, nothing implies power more than a battlegroup parked in orbit," he grinned.

"Quite. There is something else and I know you won't like it," she said seriously, "I could do with you being the official representative at the peace talks on Kerberos."

General Rivers looked at her impassively. His protests were easy to gauge, he was a combat veteran and military leader, not a politician. He fidgeted before replying.

"I'm sure you can work out where my opinions on this matter lie?"

"Indeed. Nonetheless I need a senior commander who is respected by both the military and civilians. Your defence of religious buildings seven years ago will undoubtedly be remembered by the more militant on Kerberos, and perhaps help in the negotiations. I have already checked the details of the talks and there will be representatives from all the colonies and outposts in Proxima, as well as the leaders of the major industries in the sector plus a dozen more from the religious factions and paramilitary groups."

"Admiral, what exactly are you hoping I will be able to achieve at such a gathering?"

"Well, as for political organisation, they can decide to do whatever they want. Our duty is to protect the Confederacy and to ensure that the legitimacy of the Confederate Armed Forces is adhered to throughout the colonies."

"What if they attempt concessions to the religious factions, primarily those on Prime?" asked the General.

"That is nothing to do with us. It isn't the role of the Armed Forces to interfere in the affairs of the colonies, only to act to protect our citizens and the structure of the Confederacy. The Santa Cruz and her escorts are already setting course for Kerberos, I suggest you transfer there. I understand proceedings are due to take place in the next twenty-four hours at Yama. You will have full command of the forces around Kerberos, including the communication and intelligence facilities as well as the marines."

"I...don't understand, Admiral. You are staying here and you want me to assume control of our forces at Kerberos? In these circumstances wouldn't it be better for us to stick together?"

Admiral Jarvis turned her head in disagreement.

"Under normal circumstances I would completely agree with you. However we have multiple problems that cannot be dealt with by moving our forces to Kerberos. Right now I need our troops given full medical aid and reinforcement at Kerberos. Until this is done the entire battlegroup will be a spent force. As an added bonus, by placing the marine transports and escorts in orbit, it will provide a handy reminder to the talks on the surface that the Confederate Fleet is keeping a watchful eye on proceedings."

"I understand that, Admiral, but you are not planning on joining the Fleet in orbit at Kerberos?" he asked in a confused tone.

Admiral Jarvis adjusted the tactical display to show the ship dispositions in the Proxima System. She pointed to the large gas giant Khimaira that was surrounded by a number of stations and outposts.

" I will be taking the rest of the Fleet to assemble at the navigation point off Khimaira. As you know we have a naval refuelling and supply outpost there. I am assembling all capital ships and their escorts to assemble. Smaller vessels will maintain their current operations, especially those involved in anti-piracy and installation defence. I have heard rumours of dissent in some of the crews of the squadrons based at Orthrus and Agora. By bringing the Fleet together I can isolate those that are suspect. It is my intention to root out any threats and quickly. My single biggest concern is that small groups might try and split off when they are needed, even worse they might even turn on us."

The Admiral turned from the display and looked

directly at the General, her face impassive, but resolute.

"It is imperative that by the time the talks on Kerberos are over we have the entire Fleet secure, loyal and ready to assist in whatever decision is made. One thing I can promise you is this, the crisis is not over, not by a long shot."

* * *

Spartan stood outside Captain Mathews' door and paused before knocking. His heart was pounding as he imagined all kinds of terrible scenarios that could involve Teresa, terrorists, combat or even medical problems. Last time he'd seen her was when she was still in the sickbay after having had additional surgery to her shoulder. Spartan was familiar with how operations could go wrong and the idea of infections or other complications weighed heavily on his mind. Unable to wait any longer he lifted his hand to knock but the door swung open to reveal the Captain.

"Sergeant, come in," he said as he beckoned inside his quarters.

Spartan stepped inside but couldn't contain himself.

"Is she alright?"

The Captain shut the door and turned to face him. "She's fine. Please sit, we need to talk."

The room was a modest affair but much better than the quarters the enlisted men had to use. There were three chairs to one side and a bunk running along the far wall. The Captain indicated a chair to Spartan before sitting down himself. Spartan sat down, at least partially placated that nothing terrible had happened.

"I didn't realise that you and Private Morato were so close," he said as he watched Spartan.

"We've become good friends since well before Kronus, Sir. Last I heard she was still recovering from her wounds. Where is she?"

"Okay, that is the question isn't it? First of all, her recovery is going well. She isn't fully healed but is certainly well enough to return to non-combat based duties. I'm afraid that she isn't on board the ship though."

"Where is she?" demanded Spartan, now starting to feel a little agitated.

"As I said, she is okay. She has joined a reconnaissance patrol and will be back in about a week. It is a routine op but I'm sure you appreciate that for reasons of OPSEC I cannot go any further. I couldn't even if I wanted to. I'm not privy to the information either. I know you want you know more but that's all I can offer."

"Why her? I don't understand, Sir. Surely the battalion has trained reconnaissance units for that kind of work?"

"That is all I know. Who knows, maybe she has certain skills? Maybe it was an emergency and there were no other units on board. In the end it doesn't matter, she's gone for a short time and will be back upon completion of her mission."

Spartan said nothing, he was evidently lost in thought and the Captain had neither the time nor the inclination to turn the discussion into something resembling a social conversation. He decided to revert to something Spartan always seemed more comfortable with.

"Tell me about the CES suits and New Carlos? I have a report due from Lieutenant Daniels, but I'd like to hear from you."

Spartan looked about the room as he gathered his thoughts.

"Well, initially they performed well. The modifications fitted by the technicians proofed them against most small arms fire. Once in combat the weapons were adequate for most of the tasks we used them for. There were some problems with the suits, mainly to do with speed and size," he started.

"Tell me about their battlefield effectiveness? How significant were they, let's say against an equivalent number of marines in PDS suits?"

"There is no comparison, Sir. When we were hit, the marine line almost broke several times. The CES units were able to hold the line against overwhelming numbers. Their increased firepower and ability to take damage meant they could hold where three times their number would have been needed. At close range they are vastly superior. The enhanced power in close combat allows one man to take on several shock troopers."

"Okay, that is promising. What about the problems, then?"

"The single biggest weaknesses were durability and size. With them being modifications of our basic gear, we still suffered from gaps in armour and several exposed critical systems. The size makes them easier to spot and hit with heavy weapons. Several took direct missile strikes, though I saw at least one lose a limb and keep going. There is also the longevity issue. At the end of just over a day's worth of fighting most of the suits had broken down or been made unusable due to damage, fatigue or failure."

"So how would you sum them up for use by the battalion?"

"Well, Sir, I think Lieutenant Daniels would be the best person to answer that question."

Captain Mathews smiled inwardly, noticing the deference to Spartan's new commanding officer and also that a level of respect must now exist between them. It was a given fact in the battalion that units meshed together best when flung together in difficult times.

"Indulge me, I'd like to hear your opinions, from a sergeant's point of view."

"Okay. In my opinion the CES suits offer the equivalent of light armour or tanks for the marines. They give us a piece of heavy protection that can assist in the assault of objectives or to provide mobile defensive positions, as at

New Carlos. They excel in close combat however, that is where their strength, power and firepower can be used more effectively. They are too vulnerable and resource intensive for normal operations. If we all used them we would have half the battalion out of action in a few days, Sir."

Captain Mathews nodded as he listened to Spartan. He was very interested in the development of the weapon system and Spartan's comments would be of help for his plans.

"Based on these experiences, I am intending on pushing command for the option for the requisition of more of the suits from Fleet stores for conversion to a number of roles. I would appreciate your assistance in their development, if you're interested?"

"Definitely, I think with additional modifications we can produce a piece of equipment that will make the battalion even more powerful and effective than before."

"Excellent. Now, there is another more pressing matter and again one in which I could really use your help," he said with a hint of intrigue to his voice.

"Let me guess, you've found something and you need a team to investigate?" asked Spartan with a smile.

"Not quite, actually, it concerns Kerberos."

"Kerberos, the industrial world? What is going on there, Sir?"

"That is a very good question. As you know there are

peace talks and negotiations over some kind of Colonial settlement in this sector. The negotiations range on all topics from religious freedoms to changes to the electoral process, it even goes up to the autonomy of some colonies from what I hear."

"What does any of that have to do with us?"

The Captain looked a little uncomfortable, perhaps surprised by the speed in which Spartan had identified the crux of the problem.

"For the most part you are correct, it has nothing to do with the military. That is providing nothing changes with respect to the sovereignty of colonies or the basic structure of the Confederacy. We are sending a representative from the military to stand by any decision or to ask any questions that are relevant to the military command."

Spartan looked at him, waiting expectantly for some kind of a punch line, then it dawned on him.

"You want me to be the representative?" he asked incredulously.

"You?" he laughed.

Spartan looked a little taken aback.

"You have many sterling qualities, Sergeant, but diplomacy probably isn't one of them. No, what I need is your experience, your instincts and if required, your fighting skills. I want you to be our representative's personal guard on the planet."

"Me? Who would I be guarding, Sir?"

"General Rivers, head of the Marine Corps forces in this sector."

"I don't understand, Sir. Yes, it is a great honour, but why me? We have many more experienced marines on board, I can vouch for many of them..." he started before the Captain raised his hand.

"There are already enough guns there from multiple groups, each with different agendas. I have been tasked this duty by the Admiral herself and she wants me to deal with it outside of the normal channels. I need somebody that hasn't been in the Corps too long and the Zealots, or whoever else is involved, might already have their claws into. There is a chance the situation could get dicey down there and if that happens, well, we need someone used to handling things a little differently to the way we do. You are unpredictable and your close quarter combat skills are reportedly the best in the battalion."

Spartan said nothing, he felt as though yet another bomb had exploded nearby. Since arriving at the Titan Naval Station he seemed to be thrown from one operation to the next without a chance for a break, rest or to even try and order the events in his mind. At this rate he thought his head might actually explode!

"Will I have a team?"

"There will be a Marine Guard Unit on the shuttle and the Confederate Guard's Company will as always provide personal protection for all official Council members.

When on the planet the Kerberos military will provide an honour guard for the General. An additional combat unit from the Santa Cruz would be considered a major snub to their forces. It is best if we keep our numbers to the minimum."

"I could do with an extra pair of eyes on an assignment like this," Spartan replied, his voice implying it was more a request than a suggestion.

"I see. Who did you have in mind?"

"Well, Marcus Keller, one of the privates from the Santa Maria came back with the rest of our unit. He has seen some rough action and I know I can trust him."

"I'll check him out prior to the mission, if he is okay you can have him. One last thing, you will be travelling with a third person, Lieutenant Carter. He's a member of the Personal Protection Unit on the Santa Cruz, but knows nothing about our little conversation. He is trustworthy as far as any marine officer is and the operation will be conducted under his command, anything else could look suspicious. Just remember, the only person you need to look after is the General, and the only person you can trust is yourself. Now, Carter is already with the General and briefing him on the operation."

"Understood, Sir." Spartan paused, considering the enormity of the responsibility he would be undertaking, "I should probably go and see the General then."

Captain Mathews turned his head in disagreement.

"No, let Carter have a few hours to get settled in. It's important he feels its his operation. General Rivers is aware of your role and if push comes to shove, he will defer to you, not the Lieutenant." There was just a hint of a question in the statement.

"I think I understand, Sir. How long before we reach Kerberos?"

"From our current position out here we will be there in about twenty hours. Enough time to get some rack time. That sounds like a good idea, remember, trust nobody!"

CHAPTER EIGHT

Ten years prior to the uprising on Proxima the first of the colonisation fleets were sent. These three fleets were massive undertakings, each one taking years to assemble and thousands of tonnes of materials to build. It was always the intention of the Confederacy to continue expansion and the foundation of new colonies on Epsilon Eridani, Gliese 876 and Procyon were part of the long term strategy to help spread mankind amongst the stars.

The New Colonies

Spartan lay in his bunk, his body aching and his mind crying out for a few hours rest. Try as he might, sleep avoided him. The bizarre nature of his latest mission still worried him, the twists and turns of the short briefing he had with Captain Mathews had created more questions than answers for him. On the one hand he had been chosen, well, apparently chosen, to help protect the General. On the other being officially seconded to a lieutenant he'd never heard of, but wasn't to trust. The talks were already underway between the Council members present in the Proxima System and various military organisations and departments were providing security. He had read and re-read the organisational charts and was still confused as to the jurisdiction of each section. As he understood it, each colony in the Confederacy returned between one and three councillors depending on their size. These councillors represented the colonies at all gatherings of the Council and for the voting on all decisions that affected the colonies. In this sector the Assembly Building on Kerberos was one of the potential locations that could be used to assemble the Proxima councillors for debate and discussion. A similar assembly could be convened in Alpha Centauri, though decision in one sector had to be ratified in the other for them to be valid. With no contact with the old world colonies, it appeared Proxima was looking to resolve these problems alone.

He thought about the old worlds in Alpha Centauri. He'd never been to them, they were a long way away and unless a citizen had the funds or was in the military, you were unlikely to ever visit them. What did intrigue him was that the Alpha Centauri colonies were over a hundred years older than anything in this sector. Their planets were better developed and the military forces more substantial and capable. As expected the politics and society of the old worlds was more conservative and far less tolerant of some of the more left wing organisations and religions that had tried to flex their muscles over the years. The formation of the Confederacy some ninety-eight years ago was supposed to have removed the heavy-handed rule of the old worlds. It was to be replaced with a more open, tolerant system of mutually independent colonies held together by an agreement of law, trade and defence. At least, that was what he had learned at school. His experience in the last few years had shown him that many people in the new colonies had a strong distrust of the Confederacy or in fact anybody outside of their own colony. Quite how this affected his mission he wasn't sure. In the end he decided to concentrate on this one job, protection of the General. He would leave the rest to anybody that could be interested.

As he tried to forget about what was to come, he then found he was unable to shake off his experiences of the combat on Prime. In the past he'd been involved in many fights, some of them for money, others to just stay alive, but nothing could have prepared him for the violence he had just witnessed. Every time he closed his eyes the sounds and smells of the battle flooded back to him. The room was dark, lit only by the dull red lights that marked the bulkhead and hatches out of the room. Opposite him the bulk of Marcus, the massive German marine he'd met months ago, was fast asleep. There were two other marines in the room but Spartan couldn't remember their names. The events had been so extreme he was starting to lose track of people, even time. He sat up and reached out to the water canteen near the bunk. It was lukewarm but still quenched his thirst.

He had spoken in private with Marcus about the mission but he didn't seem particularly inspired by the news. In fact he'd just listened in agreement before heading to his bunk for sleep. Spartan could only imagine either the man was exhausted or that he didn't care where he was sent. Of all the people he knew on the ship, Marcus was the most dependable in a fight. He would have chosen Tex next if he'd been allowed more in his team, but Mathews had insisted that the bodyguard unit had to be no more than three people. In some ways Spartan felt he had been given a major honour, but if anything went wrong on Kerberos the life of the most senior marine officer in the entire sector would be in his hands.

He looked at the clock on the wall. He had another four hours before he needed to be ready to meet the General and his team to go over the final details of the operation. He considered getting up and ready before a stabbing pain in his temple told him he needed to drink more water and rest a little. One more sip and he dropped back to the bed, he was asleep almost as soon as his head hit the pillow.

* * *

The Assembly Building was the official debating chamber for the Kerberos Colony and also one of the locations used by the Proxima Council when critical decisions had to be made. Since the founding of the Confederacy it had been used in this context only three times, even then it was just to clarify and then vote on decisions already made by the Council in Alpha Centauri based on Terra Nova. It was large and comprised of three rectangular buildings situated around a circular rotunda that lifted up above the structure. It was made of pale stone and the inside was adorned with sculptures and artworks of the birth of the colony over two hundred years ago and more recently, the Great War and the creation of the Confederacy that had followed it. The Centre Chamber, the largest occupied part of the building, was made up of three layers of seating in a wide circle, creating enough space for up to a hundred representatives.

The design was intended to cope with all the colonial members from the many planets, moons and station colonies in the Proxima Star System. Normally it would be made up of the local members of the Kerberos Assembly but today it was packed with most of the sector officials or their representatives. The fighting on Prime was a terrible event. Most of the members were keen to voice their concerns and do what they could to facilitate an agreement to stop the fighting and unrest that had already torn Prime apart. There were also the unresolved issues of the secular colonies that had plagued many of the colonies for years, in one or two cases going back to the actual founding of the Confederacy after the Great War.

Inside the main Assembly Building almost a hundred people were listening to a speech by President West of Kerberos, who was also one of the three councillors from the Kerberos Colony. He had been one of the key drivers behind some kind of a peace agreement. He'd also made a great deal of the fact that the Assembly would be convened to come to a long lasting and equitable arrangement between the colonies and their respective belligerent factions. Normally the meeting would be run by the Speaker but today was a special occasion, the first to ever take place in the colony under the authority of President West. For something this important the President had needed to take personal control.

* * *

Light was fading in Yama City and as often happened the coolness of the night was amplified by the light patter of rain on the stone walkways of the new city. The city lights were garish, most coming from the downward facing street lighting. A substantial amount also came from the many lights and equipment set up by the scores of news crews and reporters that had arrived for the momentous event.

As the groups outside continued chanting, those inside prepared for the critical gathering. The leaders of Proxima's colonies and the many other groups were still in closed session inside the massive structure. A number of video screens and speaker systems were already being erected so that the people in the rain could see what was happening inside. So far only two of the great screens were in position and although one kept crackling the second showed a clear picture of the hall. Around this display a number of at least fifty people pushed and shoved for a better look.

The cold and wet the weather seemed to do little to dampen the enthusiasm of the Kerberos citizens. The stoic members of the public stood outside the Colonial Assembly Building waving their placards and shouting in support of their representatives. Most of them outside were common citizens, many of whom toiled in the factories and industries covering the surface of the single planetary colony. Scores of them wore masks or filter tubes in their nostrils to help with the lower oxygen content of the atmosphere. Though Kerberos was one of the newer colonies it was wealthy. But the crowds in the streets appeared not to have benefited from the massive increases in trade and production in the last thirty years. At least a dozen people carried placards from the new Socialist Worker Party that aimed to improve the lot of those working in the heavy industries. They advocated common ownership and cooperative management of the means of production and allocation of resources in the colony. Another group from one of the lesser-known Disciples of Christ decried the breakdown in morality of the colonies and pushed their own arguments of piety, absolution and belief in the old idea of the Trinity.

Most of the placards complained about simple domestic matters such as job security, cuts in social spending and the profits of the mega corporations that did most of their work on the planet. One group stood out more than the rest. About thirty members of the Church of Echidna had assembled around an icon of the half woman half-snake goddess they worshipped. The icon was a bizarre fusion of monotheism and pagan mythology. It was the largest church on Kerberos but so far no religious groups had been given access to the Assembly. One man in the traditional robes of the Church pushed ahead and moved up the marble steps to the entrance of the building. Alongside him were three men in hooded robes, it was not clear who they were as their clothing covered their faces. A line of riot police blocked his path.

"You can't come in, only Colonial and Confederate representatives," said the officer in charge.

"I am an official representative of the Church of Echidna, our presence has been requested at the Assembly," the man said.

The officer looked down at his datapad, checking the details of those with permission to move through the barrier. It took a few seconds and as the wait dragged on a few more of the Church members moved forward carrying the icon with them.

"I have you and three assistants on the list, you can come through," the officer moved aside to let the man and his three assistants in.

As they moved forward the people with the icon tried to follow them into the building.

"Hey, that thing has no business in the Assembly!" shouted somebody in the crowd.

"They have the right to enter!" shouted another.

A substantial number with placards starting shouting their support for the Church followers, some even pushed ahead to help protect the icon. At the same time angry disagreements spread like wildfire through the crowd.

"Barrier!" A police officer shouted to the rest of his men.

The police responded quickly and in less than twenty seconds the loose groups of officers formed up into a tight line of armour and shields. Their state-of-the-art body armour produced full head, torso and limb protection. Each of them wore additional plating around the important joints and organs. The hardened black armour gave them the appearance of giant beetles, an impression that was reinforced by their oversized helmets. As well as providing around the head defences the helmets were equipped with drop down shoulder and neck protection against overhead blows and missile strikes. This should be enough protection against all but military grade weapons, but that didn't stop each of them from carrying a large transparent rectangular shield. They were slightly concave to provide additional strength and rigidity, the marks and scratches along their fronts easily demonstrated their frequent use. Facing outwards the armour provided a powerful and secure barrier to protect the Assembly and the important dignitaries inside.

In the commotion someone near the icon started to scream. It wasn't obvious who it was but a number of people starting to run about and a few fell over. Sergeant Travis, on the watch for potential problems, gave a quick hand signal to his officers. Some of them were unable to see him due to the number of protestors pushing up to the line. Already they were starting to push and shove against the armoured line.

"We have a situation at the icon, Charlie Squad secure the icon and its group. Help them inside the line," he said into the intercom link fitted into his helmet.

Almost instantly half a dozen policemen broke from the line and surged ahead towards the icon. A few of the protestors thought they were the intended objective and tried to stop them from passing. As two of the men dealt with the immediate problem, the other four police officers pushed their way to the icon, but it was too late. With a flash the icon and a dozen of the followers disappeared. The effect was as though a massive rock had been dropped into a pond. The immediate area around the icon was engulfed in a featureless void that swiftly turned into an angry cloud of pressure and debris. The massive blast ripped through the crowd, the shockwave knocking many to the ground and sending dirt, blood and debris in every direction. Those nearest to the blast were torn to pieces and the ones just a short distance away suffered terrible wounds and burns. The blast was so powerful it managed to catch a handful of the police who were closest, even managing to rip the helmets and shields from the first two. One of the officers, a man called Harris and the oldest of the riot police, took the brunt of the blast onto his chest's body armour. Incredibly none of the debris penetrated but the power of the blast catapulted him twenty metres through the air and into the street, where he landed hard on his back. The entire area around the building erupted into screams and shouting as people who could walk did their best to escape the scene. Their running turned to panic and in moments the scene became one of chaos.

Sergeant Travis, leader of the police unit lifted himself from the ground and wiped the dust from his visor. As he stood he found himself engulfed in a thick cloud that obscured his vision. He looked back to see one of his men on his back with a piece of metal embedded in his chest.

The man had obviously died from the violent impact.

"Sergeant Travis, we have an incident here, explosive device at the Southern entrance to the Assembly Building. Officers down, civilians wounded. Need ATU and medical assistance immediately!"

"Understood, aerial medical unit inbound, ETA seven minutes," came the reply.

The Sergeant moved along to check on the rest of his unit. Luckily the armour and shields of the men had protected them from the worst of the attack but there were still many injuries. He walked towards three of his men as one was wrapping a cloth around a bleeding wound on his leg.

"Gardner, get the rest of your squad down to the street level. We need this area cordoned off. Jenkins!" he shouted.

He waited for a moment before his redoubtable second in command appeared.

"What is your status?" asked Sergeant Travis.

"I've got four injured, they are being taken care of now, luckily nothing too serious. The three squads from the Ninth Precinct are unhurt, I'm still checking on the rest."

"Good, good. Get the three units down to the street fast! We need medical attention for the injured. Keep one squad back to protect the Assembly."

As he watched the dust cloud started to settle revealing over twenty bodies plus more people still staggering away from the crowd. In the middle of the bodies were the charred remains of the religious standard. Incredibly it was still intact but had suffered damage and scorch marks from the attack. Around the damaged icon were the bodies of the members of the Church, each one dressed in their traditional garb and all badly mutilated by the blast. From the boundaries of the area small groups of people emerged, some were bleeding, others may have just arrived. At the sight of the partially burnt icon they started to swoop back in as bodies were still being carried away.

"Cordon off the icon, get those people away from there!" he shouted.

Sergeant Travis moved down from the line and towards the relic, doing his best not to slip and fall on the blood. Small numbers of police joined him as they tried to create a protective screen around the clump of bodies by the relic.

A man lifted a stick in the air and waved it over his head.

"Zealots out, Zealots out!" he cried before being dragged down by the mob.

Travis tried to push his way through to the man, but was too late as he was already being dragged off by four burly men, who then promptly disappeared into the darkness.

"Dispatch, we need that backup now. The Assembly Building is not secure, I repeat the Assembly is not secure!" he said firmly into his radio.

There was no response from the set. He tried again but

the numbers of people moving back into the area was just too much, with a hand signal he instructed his men to fall back to their original positions outside the building. As they moved back the crowd plucked and grabbed at the ruined icon, though whether for souvenirs or as relics he couldn't tell.

Jenkins rushed over to him.

"Sir, we've got a problem around the corner. A car has been crashed into our command centre and a device set off. They managed to get everybody out but they have had to fall back to the Assembly perimeter. Something big is going on here!"

* * *

"Fellow representatives, as you are all aware, in the last year events have conspired to bring violence and disorder to the colonies of the Confederation. The causes are many and in some cases are still being discovered. In calling this Assembly it is my hope that we can rebuild the road to real peace and lasting security throughout the sector. We can be strong, safe and productive if we work together. I am fully aware that there have been two previous attempts to resolve the grievances between the religious organisations on Prime and the political structures of the Confederacy. They both failed and it is now our job as citizens of the Confederacy to ensure we do more than lay out another road map. We owe this to every man, woman and child in the sector!"

A round of applause spread gently through the building. It was hardly the resounding roar he may have hoped for but it was at least audible. There was always the possibility he would have been shouted down and that would have been a disaster. As the noise dulled he prepared to continue.

"Starting today…" he said before being interrupted by the first bomb blast.

From inside the substantial stone building the explosion sounded like a dull thud but it was clear something bad, if nothing else by the number of security officials rushing to the doors and balconies to see what was happening.

"Please be calm, we are checking on this disturbance. Stay where you are, there is no cause for alarm," the President said in a reassuring voice.

The sound of alarms was barely audible and the sound of police hovercraft flying over the building was hard to disguise. The recognisable blare of police sirens ran from one side of the building to the other as more police vehicles swept in around the building. A police officer hurried around the outer walkway of the hall until he reached the President, he leaned in and spoke briefly before handing him a datapad. The President looked at it for a moment, the officer headed back as the President stood up to speak. Some of the representatives started to get up, either to see what was happening or to try and find safer surroundings.

"Please be calm, this situation will be dealt with shortly. I have just received this report from the local police officers providing security for this important gathering. It is believed that an unknown attacker has triggered an explosive device in the crowd. There have been many casualties but it is unknown whether they or this Assembly was the intended target," he said sternly.

One of the door burst open along the lower side of the hall and in ran three men, each of them dressed in drab grey overalls and carrying a bloodied body between them. A number of security people ran to stop them. They weren't fast enough to prevent the first man from speaking.

"It was the police, they killed the Echidna representatives in the street…in cold blood!" the man shouted before he was dragged to the ground.

As the security men tried to restrain him one of the men managed to fight free and pushed out into the middle of the hall. In one hand he carried an object, it looked like a small metal ball about the size of a man's fist. Several people spotted his movement and started shouting, assuming it was a bomb. He was evidently about to speak or do something with the item when one of the guards jumped forward and struck him with his baton. It was a heavy strike and intended to hit the man in the arms but in the struggle he was struck in the temple. In an instant the man collapsed to the ground, blood running from the wound to his head.

As he hit the floor the object dropped from his hand and rolled into the crowd. Some of the spectators ducked down behind their seats but the rest stared on intently, fascinated by the spectre of what might be. As the object stopped they could see it presented no real threat.

"What is it?" shouted one.

"A snake or something, a figurine," said another.

Muttering and shouting spread before a man in the robes of the Church of Echidna stepped inside. Several of the dignitaries bowed as he passed, showing due reverence to the leader of the Church on Kerberos. The man moved out into the open area. As he approached the fallen object the security guards stepped back. Either they had been ordered to back off or they could see the situation for what it was.

"Order!" shouted the President but it was no good.

Pandemonium erupted in the hall with officials from each of their worlds trying to get a better view of what was going on. One of the trade representatives turned and quickly left and was followed by a small number of followers to the nearest emergency exit. At the same time two guards in dark suits and armed with carbines approached the President, flanking him on both sides to protect him from any potential threats.

"Delegates, please be seated, this disturbance will be dealt with shortly!"

The robed man stopped and knelt down to pick up the object. As he held it the people attempting to leave the building turned and watched. From outside a number of shouts and cries could be heard, presumably from the gathering protests. The man lifted up the object and turned to face the President.

"President, this is part of the Icon of Echidna, the ancient relic of our religion and our most revered symbol. We intended to present the icon to the Assembly as a sign of our respect to the people of Yama City. Sadly it appears this is the only part of the relic that has not been destroyed by the fires of violence or of the greed of material gain. I, the Bishop of Yama, offer this small piece of Echidna to the proceedings," he said before walking to the small altar at the back of the room. He placed it down carefully. A number of the delegates started to clap and more than a dozen men shouted and cheered him.

Behind him the security units dragged these other men away and out through a small doorway to the side of the building. It was standard procedure, after all, they were not allowed inside the hall. But from where the delegates sat it looked as though the security forces and police were beating or arresting people at will.

Ambassador Drusilla from Orthrus stood from her seat and spoke out through the loudspeaker system, her anger obvious.

"This is intolerable. We were told this was an open debate between representatives of the colonies and all the religious groups. These attacks on our brothers in the Church of Echidna will not go unpunished! Your state lackeys are attacking legitimate protesters outside!" she cried.

The Ambassador sat down, giving a brief glance to her opposite number from the Agora colony. Shouting and arguments spread through the many groups inside the building. The President tried to placate them but it was too little, too late. He might be the President of this colony but in the Assembly there were plenty of factions who considered him nothing more than a regional puppet. The ambassador for Agora pressed the button in front of his seat to indicate he would like to speak to the Assembly.

"As the elected representative of Agora I would like to ask the Bishop of Yama to offer his thoughts and considerations on the problem in the Confederacy. I think it might be useful to hear some free speech and discussion away from the politics of this chamber," he said in a sarcastic manner.

A chorus of agreement echoed from some of the people inside, even so a number declined to join in, some even turning their heads in disagreement.

The Bishop lifted his hand to thank those who wished to hear him speak. As he stood the Assembly quietened down, each curious to hear what the most important religious figure in the colony had to say.

* * *

The shockwave from the shuttle rippled past the craft as it emerged into the atmosphere. Now travelling at thousands of miles per hour the heat from the massive amount of friction superheated the ceramic plates fitted along the hull of the craft. This was always the most dangerous part of landing forces planet-side. Just one break in the ceramic plates and the hot gasses would tear inside the craft, melting away the metal alloys and vaporising the vessel in a matter of seconds.

"Can't we go faster?" asked an irritable General Rivers.

"ETA eleven minutes, Sir, any faster and we'll burn up on re-entry," explained the co-pilot.

The marine assault shuttle was one of the standard craft from on board the CCS Santa Cruz. Like many of the vessels in the battlegroup, it showed the marks and scars of battle from the last week. This particular shuttle had sustained over a dozen bullet strikes during the evacuation at the Titan Naval Station and then debris and storm damage during the contested landings on Prime. Though most of the damage had been repaired, the paintwork was in a terrible state and one of the gun mounts on the side of the craft was still out of action. However, it was still the least damaged shuttle on the ship.

"You're that desperate to meet a load of arguing politicians?" asked Spartan.

The General smiled but looked as if he had a great deal on his mind. Spartan thought about the news he'd recently seen and was already starting to lose count of the number of factions, interests and people in the troubles. He wondered sometimes if there was some kind of hand behind it all. Surely this amount of strife didn't just come about by chance? The more he thought about it, the more he realised that his entire life seemed to consist of events that should never happen and included people he would never expect to meet. It was strange, he had only been involved in a small number of missions but was already beginning to feel like a veteran. This was his fourth assignment since the Fleet had been rushed into action. The first had been on the moon of Kronus, the second when he was part of the team that interdicted a transport trying to escape the epic space battle around the Naval Station. His most recent action on the surface of Prime had exposed him to more violence and combat than any marine could expect in an entire career. Still, at least he had been given a twelve-hour break before meeting the rest of their unit. It wasn't much but after Prime he needed a break, any break just to calm his nerves and to rest his weary body. It wouldn't be long before he met the rest of the team so they checked their communications gear, procedures and plan for the major contingencies that might occur on Kerberos. He still couldn't believe the speed of the assignments coming his way. He could only hope that upon his return he would finally get some rest. By the time he was back it couldn't be long before Teresa and her team returned to the Santa Cruz and that was a part he was really looking forward to.

"Uh, Sir, we have reports of violence outside the Assembly Building. Looks like there has been some kind of bomb attack," said the co-pilot.

"Give me that," replied the General, ever keen to get the information directly from the source.

The co-pilot handed over the datapad. A ribbon type cable kept it connected to the main computer system due to the large bandwidth required for the system and the encoding used. Unlike other datapads, this one would be useless unless connected to a main system like this one.

"What does it say?" Spartan asked looking more interested than worried.

Lieutenant Carter, still wearing his long black trench coat, had his own datapad and was busy sat in the corner as he assessed his own data feed. Spartan looked over to him, noticing how the man kept to himself and shared only the minimum with either him or the General. It might be nothing, but Spartan's instincts told him that this was a man he had no reason to trust.

"As I expected the Council meeting has been used as an excuse for any group or faction with a grudge to come out of the woodwork. It looks like a religious icon of some kind was dragged up to the perimeter outside the Assembly Building. There was at least one explosion nearby, the casualties include police officers, members of two churches and a large number of civilians."

"Why? What is the point, Sir?"

"I don't know. The only thing I do know is that it is being used as just more negative PR towards the Confederacy."

"What the fuck has this got to do with the Confederacy?" asked an irritable Marcus.

The General looked over to the man who instantly straightened, suddenly realising who he was talking to.

"Sorry, Sir," he said as he rubbed his brow.

"Incredible as it might seem but there are many in the colonies, especially those on the newer worlds like Kerberos here, where the Confederacy means subservience to a higher authority. It is nonsense of course, almost all planetary affairs are controlled by a colony's own government but that doesn't stop the public from pointing the finger. On Kerberos we are blamed for food prices, wages, morality and then when it goes wrong we're accused of brutality and intervention in colonial affairs," the General explained.

Spartan sat there, a thin grin appearing on his face.

"What's amusing you, Sergeant?"

"You, Sir, you're starting to sound like a politician already," he laughed.

"Oh…crap…that's all I need!" laughed General Rivers.

The shuttle rocked a little as it hit turbulence. From their height they could now see the lights of the city below but much of the detail was obscured by the clouds and rain. A roar from the jet engines indicated that the craft was lowering its speed as it swooped down low towards the principal military base in the colony. It was a far cry from the large naval base on the planet, but time was of the essence, and right now the General needed to get inside the Assembly before anything else bad happened.

"We're two minutes from the landing pad, please ensure your belts are fitted and don't release them till the landing light is lit in front of your seating," said the pilot over the intercom.

The craft bucked and shook again as more thick air shook it during its descent. Like most of the craft used by the Marine Corps the shuttle was designed with rotating jet nozzles so that it could perform short take off and vertical landings. It was more fuel efficient to land conventionally like an aeroplane but the smaller military base wasn't equipped with a long runway. As the engines altered their direction the forward speed of the craft altered drastically.

"What the hell is that?" Marcus was watching from the starboard window.

Lieutenant Carter shouted from his position further back and as Spartan looked a number of rounds ripped past the man, luckily managing not to hit anybody.

Spartan leaned over to see a line of yellow dots arcing out into the sky.

"Get down!" he shouted.

Without hesitating the marines pulled their heads down into the classic brace position. It wasn't a moment too soon as a dozen medium calibre machine gun rounds tore into the fuselage and blasted across the interior of the craft. Incredibly none of the fire hit the passengers, but they did manage to cause a series of flashes and sparks on one of the jet nozzles fitted to the side of the craft. The shuttle lurched to the right as the loss of power forced it to veer sharply. Another burst of fire tore a hole in the side of the craft and a great surge of air gushed out of the vessel.

"Fuck me!" shouted Spartan as he found himself being forced to the side of the craft, held into position by the sturdy straps on his harness.

"Sir, are you hurt?"

"I'm fine, where is Carter?" asked the General.

Spartan looked around the craft but he could only see Marcus, General Rivers and a red pattern across a damaged section of the aft of the vessel.

"Look's like Carter bought it," Marcus said with little hint of concern.

"We're going down, brace for impact! Mayday! Mayday! Marine Transport One is making an emergency landing!" the pilot shouted, his voice loud enough from the cockpit for the passengers to hear.

"It never bloody stops!" Spartan grabbed onto the seat, waiting for the inevitable grinding smash of the impact.

CHAPTER NINE

The rise of the Church of Echidna throughout the Confederacy saw an explosion in the worship of artefacts from the destroyed church on Terra Nova. The most revered relic of all was the icon of the entwined woman and snake. Though originally an allegory for the sins of mankind it had taken on the significance of the cross used in early Christian worship.

Holy Icons

From inside the large cockpit at the front of the Tamarisk the crew sat and watched the vessel's autopilot help navigate through the treacherous shipping lane of the Rim. Like the asteroid belt back in the old Solar System of Earth it was packed with rocks the size of small moons, debris and scores of space stations. To make matters worse the groups and companies that worked out in this part of space were constantly moving raw materials and their stations around. This had the effect of transforming the environment in a matter of months.

Special Agent Johnson and Commander Anderson were both sifting through the data collected by the dozens of scanners, ultrasonic and infrared monitors and radio traffic loggers. So far they had established that none of the seventy asteroids in sector 3G were occupied, one had been used as some kind of base in the past. There was a slight possibility there could be some data or evidence on board but according to their intelligence, whatever was happening would be taking place in person. It would therefore have to be on one of the stations. On the screens in front the three stations were shown as three-dimensional models, each with all of its surface detail modelled as a vector graphic. They were all the same size and one in particular appeared to be taking on substantially more traffic than the other two. The station off to their left was nestled in amongst a dozen asteroids and much of its power system was offline.

"Our contact is waiting on the main station, it is known as Alpha Three in this area and according to the latest Confed report it is a known place for smugglers and organised crime," said Agent Johnson.

"We should be shutting this place down, not sneaking about."

"That will come another day, Kowalski. For now the stations are assets, vital intelligence assets that we need to milk for information," said the Commander.

They sat looking at the displays, watching the movement of the shipping and containers in the area. It was like a complicated game of chess with scores of pieces moving about, far more than they could expect to track.

"We have a lot of data to track in this area, any thoughts before we proceed?" Anderson asked the rest of the crew.

Bishop answered, eager to voice his opinion.

"I don't like this area. If anything goes wrong we will have to spend over an hour on autopilot to try and force our way clear of the debris field before we can even think about pushing the engines. There's a good chance we could be cornered."

"True but if we're smart we should be able to get in and out without anybody even knowing we were there," Teresa was examining the screen.

"What about the actual meeting, where is it most likely to be in this area?" asked Anderson. "How about the Alpha Three Station?"

"No way would it be on the busy one, which would be obvious. If you look at the other two stations they are definitely trying to appear as if they're almost totally inoperative. That one," Bishop pointed to the station to their left, "is very suspicious."

Agent Johnson turned his head in disagreement, he was

obviously unimpressed with the suggestions by the crew so far.

"Well, what do you think, Johnson?" asked the Commander.

"Well, in my experience the best place to hide something is in plain view. The derelict station is the obvious place for something clandestine. If it were me, I would hold the meeting at the busiest location. It is easier to hide in a crowd and easier to escape if something goes wrong. Ever tried to sneak about on your own? If you do the same with a hundred other people you will find it a lot easier."

Bishop slowly nodded in agreement. "Yeah, actually, scrub what I just said. That makes a lot more sense. If you think about it, when we do our sniper training we never hide in the obvious place. If you are in a field with one building you set up near the building, not in it."

"I'm inclined to agree, Bishop," said Commander Anderson. "Either way we still need to land and meet our contact on the busiest station. If you're right, Sir, it will save us a lot of time," he said as he flicked a few switches on the computer console.

"I suggest you all go and get ready, we'll be landing within the hour and we have to get a move on. Remember, we are a civilian crew and we're here to arrange to sale of our goods on the black market."

The all went further back inside the craft as Anderson continued to check the data on the communication traffic throughout the Rim.

"Commander, you might want to hear this, it sounds like there's been trouble on Kerberos," said Johnson.

"Put it on."

He flicked a few switches and the inside of the craft was quickly filled with the sounds of police units coordinating their actions. The video screen at the front of the passenger section flicked on, showing four separate video feeds of the events unfolding on the surface.

* * *

Spartan looked back at the wreckage of their shuttle. The skill of the pilots was outstanding, not only had they landed safely but they'd been able to bring the shuttle down to within a hundred metres of the emergency fire tenders based at the last third of the short runway. Before they had jumped clear of the burning shuttle the tenders were already there, spraying fire retardant foam and stopping the heat from reaching the volatile fuel or ammunition stores.

General Rivers stood to one side as he checked the survivors.

"Where did the fire come from?" asked a furious Spartan.

The General said nothing, he just looked over the wreckage and then at his men.

"That was some damned good flying, guys," he shook the hands of the pilots.

He then turned back to Spartan and Marcus who were waiting each side of him with their side arms drawn, waiting for an attack. Behind them the tenders continued working on the burning wreckage. Off to the right a group of three armoured transporters drove down the runway towards them. All three were unmarked and painted in a dark grey that almost looked black in the rain.

"Get back!" Spartan ordered as he moved forwarded adopting the weaver stance with his left foot forward and right shoulder back. It was the most stable and mobile position to shoot in and allowed him a degree of movement if required.

Marcus moved up alongside him, lifting his L48 carbine pulling back the bolt to load in a round. The weapon was much more powerful than it suggested and was easily capable of tearing through the armour of even the PDS suits of the Marine Corps.

The vehicles pulled up with a screech. A clunk sound from the middle one indicated somebody was about to get out. The two men pointed their weapons in the direction of the sound, waiting for the inevitable firefight. As the door opened a small number of marines in the ceremonial armour of the 6th Marines Guards Company jumped out and moved in and around the General. Spartan had heard of the unit and recognised their flamboyant armour from some of the artwork on the Santa Maria. Much like the Praetorian Guard on Ancient Earth this elite unit operated on colonial territory only and their specific role was not of the protection of high-ranking Confederation civilians and military commanders. One of the men with sergeant's stripes on his shoulder moved forward and saluted to the General, he ignored Spartan and Marcus who blocked his path.

"General Rivers, Sergeant Jones, Commander of First Platoon, 6th Guards. We are to provide you with armoured escort to the Assembly Building!"

The General tapped his two guards on the shoulders, letting them know they could lower their weapons. He moved forward so that he was positioned in front of the Sergeant.

"These are my personal guards and they'll be staying with me."

"Understood, Sir, this way," replied the Sergeant as he pointed inside the middle vehicle.

The General followed him, Spartan and Marcus moved in quickly behind. As the three climbed up inside the belly of the thickly armoured vehicle the rest of the marines returned to the vehicle. General Rivers sat back and looked around at the number of computer screens and people inside the vehicle.

"Who attacked my shuttle and what are you doing about it?" asked the General.

"That isn't why I'm here, Sir. I've already checked and Kerberon police units are in pursuit of two vehicles, one of which they believe was responsible in shooting down your shuttle. You're lucky to be alive."

"Bullshit, Sergeant, luck had nothing to do with it. My pilots put the bird down with a dead computer system and half the jets out of action. Now tell me about the Assembly, is it still going ahead?"

The Sergeant appeared unconcerned at the outburst from the General. He turned around and pulled a wired datapad from a unit along the side of the vehicle. As he leaned towards the General they must have hit a bump in the road and he shuddered a little. He handed the pad over and then explained.

"Some of the delegates have asked for a recess until the security situation is resolved. As I understand it there's going to be a one day break while the security cordon is extended."

"Good," the General turned to Spartan.

"This may actually work to our advantage. I need time to go over the information presented to the Assembly before making my statement. This will give us a better chance to prepare for any surprises in the next few days."

With a screech the transport swerved slightly as it rounded a corner at high speed. The Sergeant looked at one of the screens before turning back to General Rivers.

"We're entering the Presidential Compound now, Sir.

If you need our assistance just call us with a Code Red Thirteen. We are no more than sixty seconds out," he was staring at Spartan.

Spartan and Marcus looked at each other before looking back at the stern face of the marine Sergeant. They couldn't work out if the man was checking for character traits or if he was just playing games. Either way it didn't matter as the vehicle came to a stop and the door was opened to reveal a line of six guards leading to the main entrance of the Presidential Palace. Spartan was out first but he had placed his sidearm back in his holster. Marcus was next, followed by the General. As they left the vehicle the three of them moved out of the rain and towards the lit entrance of the building. They passed the men and went into the foyer where a grand staircase led up into the main suites. The ground floor was decorated in exquisite marble with numerous paintings and artworks adorning the walls. Spartan was slightly distracted by all this as the figure of the President of Kerberos approached. He instantly felt out of place, but a quick glance over to Marcus reminded him that they needed to concentrate on their mission.

General Rivers moved quickly forwards and Spartan had to increase his pace to catch up with him. The General stopped in front of the President.

"Mr President," he said seriously.

The President sighed, he appeared relieved to see the arrival of the old General. What he hoped General Rivers could do Spartan could only imagine.

"General Rivers, you've arrived at a most opportune moment."

The President indicated for him to follow. The two men went through the open space and to a pair of wooden doors at the side of the room. As they stepped inside the President made to pull the door shut. Spartan pushed his foot inside so the door couldn't be closed. The President turned to the General.

"They cannot come inside, we have confidential state business we must discuss."

The General looked at him briefly before turning to Spartan.

"It's okay, just stay close. I have my bleeper," he held up the small metal cube to show him.

"As you wish, Sir, we'll wait here." Spartan was less than happy with the arrangement.

The President nodded at the two men and then closed the door. Marcus looked over to Spartan and grinned.

"Shit, man, you just know this mission is gonna turn sour."

"Yeah, why do I think you might be right?"

* * *

"Tamarisk, I have you on a landing trajectory," said the traffic controller in the bowels of the Alpha Three station.

"Roger, autopilot is locked in, we're in your hands," replied Commander Anderson.

It was a difficult approach as the large rotating station was almost impossible to land on manually. The approach had to be handled between the computer systems on both the ship and the platform. It was a tense moment, as any mistake or mechanical failure could result in the Tamarisk crashing into the structure and causing massive damage to both. Anderson was waiting inside the main hangar along with the rest of the crew. The Tamarisk was much too large to land on the station and instead would dock with one of the dozens of quays that stuck out from it. As an added bonus it meant the ship would be a safe distance from most of the people there should anything go wrong.

Teresa stood in her new garb and no matter how hard she tried to relax she just couldn't get used to the idea of her as some kind of rogue trader. When she had read the briefing material she assumed the trader was an elaborate name for a businessman in a suit. Contrary to what she had thought, the role required her to play a mixed character that included trader, pirate, gunrunner and mercenary. She wore a pair of tight black jeans that hung down low on her hips. Her midriff was bare and the skimpy top was an odd black and white striped design giving an almost metallic effect. Over this she wore a loose black leather jacket with a low-slung holster on her side. It was silly, but since putting on the clothes she had felt more exposed and certainly more noticeable, hardly qualities she could imagine that would be of use on their mission.

Agent Johnson had insisted that for them to fit in they would need a rough character that could pass as a displaced Carthago citizen, as many of them on the station were. When you heard the accent most people assumed trouble and it was one of the reasons she had tried to lose hers over the years. Agent Johnson had shown her photographs of a known bounty hunter they had apprehended six months earlier and she'd spent the last hour working on her clothes and makeup to get the right look. It wasn't perfect but it didn't need to be, just as long as they didn't look like customs or military personnel.

"Now remember your cover. You are an unregistered transport with medical supplies to sell on. You have contacts with the Santiago family on Carthago, known dealers in drugs and medical aid packages. Our contact is a fixer, he will expect about twenty percent to get you a good deal. You have to sell the Carthago crime family line or he'll think it's a customs raid. If that happens we're screwed," said the Commander.

Teresa looked at the rest of her team. The marines were dressed in their overalls, playing the part of her crew and they didn't appear overly impressed with their lot. Bishop was armed, apparently it was common to carry weapons openly on the station so to be any different would probably draw attention. On his back he wore a leather sheath that carried a heavily modified and cut down thermal shotgun. It was illegal on any colony in the Confederation.

A loud noise echoed through the ship and some of the fittings and mounts on the walls shook.

"That will be the mooring. Now remember, your first job is to fit in. If you are found out you'll be dead in seconds. Assuming you can pass off as the first, you can then concentrate on the second. Find out where the meeting is and get that information to me ASAP. As soon as I have a location I can send in our UAVs to infiltrate the place and collect data. The escape code word is blackwatch. You hear that and you are out, immediately! You got that?"

The side door started to open, as the light from inside the station began to enter the Commander retreated back inside the vessel to join Agent Johnson. The last thing they needed was for somebody like the Commander to be recognised. It was well known that Confederate Navy personnel never visited these kinds of places, at least not if they wanted to go home alive. A kind of uneasy truce existed between these badlands areas and the more civilised parts of the sector. Providing the traders and black marketeers stayed away from the main civilian shipping lanes, the Navy would stay away. Any pirate attack though could expect a response from a Navy cutter squadron. When that happened scores of people could expect to die or be sent to the hard labour camps.

The Commander vanished into the blackness of the ship. The low level lighting proved perfect for hiding in and unless teams boarded the ship he should be perfectly safe hidden away inside. The door continued to open until it revealed a small landing bay with a ramp leading down to the entry section of the station. Teresa went out with her hand on her holster. Her four crewmates stepped out behind her following in a loose group. When they were ten metres away from the craft the door behind them shut. It moved surprisingly quickly and the team was left exposed and vulnerable. They stopped for a moment and Teresa looked around, her hand on her hip near her pistol. She was looking for both the way inside and any potential trouble.

"There!" Bishop pointed to a dark area a short distance away.

He was pointing at a series of four large plates that could be metal doors. Each one was smooth and fitted with thick metal ribs adding additional rigidity to the metal.

"This is some heavy shit," said Kowalski.

"Yeah, this is much heavier than the rest of the plating. It's like the material we fit to the nose sections of our landing craft so we can land under fire. With this kind of protection you could withstand rocket and missile attacks. Put it this way, you're not getting in unless they want you in," added Barca.

"Hey, remember where you are," muttered Teresa, she

knew there could be listening devices installed in this part of the station.

For a moment she was concerned they may not be granted entry, she'd assumed they were doors but nothing happened. She looked back at her crew.

"How do we get inside?" asked Kowalski.

As if to answer his question the nearest door started to move with an agonizing grinding sound of heavy metal gearing. The door slid sideways to reveal the metre-thick alloy it was built from.

"Man, they built this place to last!" said Barca.

The door continued moving until a gap of three metres was created. A great hiss from inside sent a warm wind through their clothing as the pressure stabilised. From the lightly lit area outside the doorway it was hard to see inside the darkness of the station. Without hesitating Teresa went forwards and her crew followed her inside.

"Holy shit!" Williams said as they moved into the bustling heart of the station.

Though it looked busy on the outside nothing could have prepared them for the two-layered main walkway that ran as far as they could see. Along the sides of the walkway were stalls selling all manner of goods, from food and clothes to weapons and electronics. From where they stood there were easily two hundred people and probably as many again in the stalls and shops.

"I never knew..." Kowalski's voice was cut off by a

short man in a black suit who stopped in front of them.

"Never knew what?"

"What's it to you, little man?" asked Teresa, instantly sensing the potential threat posed by failing to fit in at such an early point.

The name is Antonius, I'm a trader here though I think you already know that. I assume you're Atia?"

Teresa looked at him for a moment. The man was well dressed and the two men stood nearby were certainly his hired muscle. She was tempted to grab him and beat the information she needed out of him, but that wasn't very subtle and also assumed he even had the information.

"Yeah, I'm Atia. I understand we have some arrangements to discuss."

The man looked at her, spending a little too much time staring at her bare midriff before returning to her face.

"I have somewhere quiet we can talk, there's no need to bring your posse with you though, you're all safe here," he said with a smile, though to Teresa it had the look of a sneer.

"I don't think so. My deal. My rules. Where I go, my crew goes," she said firmly.

The man shrugged, seemingly unperturbed by her disagreement. He turned and indicated for them to go with him. Teresa nodded to her team and they all followed.

The man moved off down the main street and past a number of the stalls before turning off to the right. There was a large space, big enough for two stalls that led to a small doorway guarded by another two men. These were wearing custom private security firm armour and both carrying L48 carbines, military issue. Teresa stopped in front of the men and stared at their gear. The short man turned back intrigued by her interest.

"A problem?" he asked.

"I'm just curious. Why do your men have military issue L48 carbines?"

"You're familiar with military hardware then?" he asked with a hint of suspicion.

"You can bet your ass I am. We've been looking for a shipment of the new L48a carbines for a customer on Prime. You got any?"

"L48a, never heard of them."

"Ah well, your loss. Shall we get to business?" asked Teresa before realising she may have overstepped her bounds.

Antonius looked at her again, his face giving little away. He turned back to the door the guards opened for him.

"This way," he beckoned and then disappeared inside.

Teresa looked around, there was of course a chance this could be a set up but they'd only find that out by going in. With a deep breath she stepped inside, her hand waiting on the holster just in case. It was a dark room, much darker than the aisle and stalls in the rest of the station. In the centre was a desk, lit by just one small light hanging from the ceiling. Antonius sat down behind the desk. From the darkness behind him were two tall men, again dressed in the best armour money could buy and armed with the illegally obtained L48 carbines. Antonius indicated that Teresa should sit down.

She lowered herself down, the other four crewmates staying behind her like a schoolyard gang waiting for a fight.

"Now, to business. Our mutual contact tells me you're interested in a trade for weapons. A risky business trading in weapons." He pulled out a cigar from one of the many drawers fitted in the desk. No one else in the room said anything and Teresa just looked at him, long and hard. She was trying to look like a hardened trader but it was really something she knew nothing about. One of the guards pulled out a lighter and as he did so Teresa and Bishop whipped out their weapons to point at Antonius. He started to laugh.

"I like your reaction, you're a little edgy though, yes?"

"And you're a little overweight, shall we cut to the chase?" said Teresa finally.

He stopped laughing and stared at her eyes, looking for something.

"No need to be rude now is there?"

He pulled out a datapad and placed it on the table.

"Here is what I have, four hundred L31 rifles and four hundred thousand rounds of ammunition. How about you, what did you bring to the table?"

Teresa thought for a moment, she knew her ship contained no goods of note, just the computer equipment, weapons and ammunition they would need for their operation. She also guessed that the station scanners had already checked the ship and had a rough idea of the amount of gear on board. At least she hoped so. She thought back to what Agent Johnson had said. The best place to hide something was in plain view.

"Nothing," she said with a smile on her face, "just information."

Antonius puffed two rings of smoke at her before removing the cigar.

"Information? This should be interesting."

* * *

The door to the anteroom opened and out walked the President, quickly followed by General Rivers. As they were going past the General slowed for a second so he could speak with Spartan.

"We've got a situation here, we are about to release a statement and I need you to be ready."

Spartan nodded but he had no idea what the rush was. Marcus joined him as they followed the pair though the main foyer and then towards a corridor. From memory Spartan thought this route led directly to the Assembly

Building, but he wasn't completely sure.

"Listen, the Bishop of Yama started a speech ten minutes ago, without the presence of the President. He says he has a proposal to solve the problems of the Confederacy and something tells me it is going to be a problem."

"I don't understand, Sir, why haven't you been allowed to speak yet?"

"Spartan, you're not the only one wondering about that. The President has sent a security team to remove the Bishop."

"Remove? Isn't that a bit risky?" asked Marcus.

"He has a point, with all the cameras in the Assembly it will look like he is being silenced," Spartan added.

"Perhaps, it isn't my call though."

They moved into the main Assembly Building through one of the doorways on the higher level. As expected the Bishop was addressing the crowd. Luckily the President seemed to have done the sensible thing and hadn't sent his security forces to remove him. He did however go to his own podium and gave the signal to cut the amplification to the Bishop. As the electrical system lost power, the Bishop's voice continued but at a greatly diminished volume.

"I apologise for interrupting but this session is supposed to be closed until the security situation is resolved," said the President.

Some of the representatives started to shout and complain at the sudden removal of the Bishop's platform. One even went so far as to try and gain entrance to the media booth to reactivate the audio system. One of the guards pushed her back and a small scuffle broke out.

"Mr President, I meant no disrespect. Some of the delegates asked to hear my thoughts on the current predicament and as a man of morality and faith I felt compelled to speak. Perhaps we should all go outside to discuss this if we are not welcome in this chamber?"

A great chorus or shouting and anger erupted among the members still present. Almost half of the representatives that were present during the explosions had left. The Bishop lifted his hand, calling for silence and incredibly those in the room did as he requested. General Rivers had already assessed the situation and decided to strike fast before the opportunity was lost. He walked down to the podium being used by the Bishop and pushed out his hand to shake the Bishop's.

With a forced smile the Bishop took his hand. "Bless you, my son," he said.

"Thank you, Bishop. I'm sure many here would like to hear you speak, as would I," he said as he turned to the cameras.

"I do have an urgent message on behalf of Admiral Jarvis of the Confederate Navy, who is also the senior representative of the Confederacy in this sector. Once I have conveyed this message I'm sure the President will be able to get the Assembly back on course for discussion."

The Bishop looked a little irritated at the interruption but with so many cameras now pointing at the two men he appeared to give ground. Perhaps sensing it would be a good idea to get this out of the way rather than spend the time having a publicised debate. He stepped to one side and looked off to the side of the room where a number of the Church members were seated. He turned back, his face already changing to an expression of anger. He lifted his hands and pushed the General back and away from the podium.

"Admiral Jarvis has brought death and destruction upon our people. The good citizens of Proxima have for too long been worked to the bone for the benefit of your Admiral and your precious Confederacy. Today we have a proposal that will improve the lives of our citizens forever and it will start by the dissolution of the Confederacy!" he shouted.

General Rivers stood in silence, completely surprised by the outburst from the apparently calm and collected Bishop. Spartan had already stepped forward to ensure no one else came too close to the General and guards for the Bishop did the same. A great commotion came from the side of the room as black armoured guards rushed and in and surrounded the Bishop. The President walked to the podium, flanked by his own guards though with so many armed men it was starting to give a very dark and dangerous impression.

"Bishop, General Rivers, I suggest we keep this discussion for tomorrow when the Assembly convenes," he said, trying to stay as neutral as he could manage.

With a flick of his wrist the security units moved in on the Bishop and forcibly pulled him from the podium. As soon as he started to struggle, the cameras and press were on him. As they tried to get closer a number of the guards did the same with the press and in less than five minutes the building was empty of all but the most die hard supporters of the President. He was still stood at the podium, surrounded by his guards.

"Mr President, that is not what I wanted," said General Rivers.

"Neither did I, but this Bishop has been preaching an end to capitalism and an end to secularism for the last decade. He cannot and must not been given a platform to continue his message of hate."

"I understand, you do realise this is going to get a lot worse?"

"How can it get any worse, General?"

The General shook his head. "Are you serious, Mr President? In my experience things can always get worse, a lot worse. If you want to control this thing you need to diffuse the platform he has built for himself. Announce something substantial that will make his sermons appear impotent. Whatever you do though, do it fast!"

"Come with me, I think I need a drink right now!" said the President.

General Rivers sighed as he realised the President wasn't likely to do anything significant in the next few hours. The President started to walk away when an advisor approached and started whispering to him. General Rivers, sensing it was important moved closer.

"Yes?" asked the advisor.

"Don't you 'yes' me! What is the problem?" demanded the General.

The President nodded to his advisor, giving him the go ahead to speak.

"Well, General, we're getting information from the public network stream that the church of Echidna is going to make an announcement prior to the opening of the Assembly Building tomorrow morning. They say it will change Kerberos and Proxima forever and we can expect a demonstration of their power."

"Power? Pah!" snorted the President. "This is just more rhetoric, we've had this for years now. Their announcement will be just another social programme or more likely, an attempt to reclaim their tax concessions for the Church."

"Sir, the stream indicated that a large number of groups will..." started his advisor before being cut off.

"Look, Wilkins, I'm getting a little bored with these people. Notify the security staff and report back to me at five thirty in the morning. Let them have their talks and streams. It will keep them busy while we get ready to deal with the real problems tomorrow. There are more important issues at stake than one Church!" He stomped off along with his guards.

"Idiot!" muttered General Rivers to himself before turning to Spartan.

"I need a secure link to Admiral Jarvis and fast, something is coming and if I'm right we're going to need one hell of a plan to get around it."

He acknowledged the General as he watched the President disappear around the corner, still complaining as he went.

* * *

The early morning light had already started to burn through the cloud cover when the Bishop and his entourage arrived outside of the Assembly Building. The crowds had increased overnight and they now numbered in the thousands. Most were there to hear the message from the Bishop about improvements to their lives and the promises the Church had made in the last few hours. A token number of police were scattered along the perimeter of the Assembly Building. At first glance it looked like a soft hand with regards to policing, in reality most of the riot police were deployed within the compound waiting for the word to move to where they were needed most. Mixed in with the crowd were the scores of press, some with cameras, others with microphones and all waiting for the word from the single most important person on Kerberos that day, the Bishop of Yama.

He stood up on top of the burnt relic of the Church, so recently damaged and scarred by a bomb attack. This ancient relic was already becoming even more important in its damaged state than it ever had been as a survivor from the Iconoclast Controversy so many years before.

"Good people of Yama. I come to you today as a humble man, a man of the Church and a man of peace. I am not here to stir up hostility or resentment. I am here to help turn your lives into those of joy and fulfilment. Let me tell you a terrible story, one of intolerance, depravity and the base desires of men in power. I am in touch with our brothers on every colony, ship and station in Proxima and they all tell me the same thing. When will they end? I tell you all, the time is coming!" he cried.

CHAPTER TEN

Titan, the old moon of Saturn was the first major body to be colonised in the earliest days of space travel. Its atmosphere and abundant resources quickly helped turn it into a hub from which many more stations and eventually colonies could be built. The computer failure of the habitation system demonstrated early on that over reliance on technology could have catastrophic consequences. Over a million people died in that terrible tragedy, one that has still never been fully explained.

The Lost World

Teresa was still sitting at the table, facing Antonius. In front of them was a datapad that contained military schematics and data on a number of pieces of equipment.

"Where did you get this?" Antonius asked as he

thumbed through the diagrams.

"You know I can't reveal my sources. Let's just say the friends I have are certainly not on good terms with the users of this kind of gear."

"And what was it you wanted?"

"That's more like it. I need six hundred metric tonnes of food and medical supplies, about the same amount you would expect on a single military resupply drop."

"Six hundred? Why do you need that much?" he asked suspiciously.

"None of your business, I have a need for that kind of aid package, if you're interested in what I have to offer, this is my price."

The man sat at the table, silent as he assessed the deal in front of him. From where Teresa sat she couldn't believe the man would go for it. Six hundred metric tonnes could buy several armoured vehicles. It all depended on how much the man wanted the data. He looked at the datapad again, looking intently at one of the items.

"This datafile has the official signature seal of the Avagana Colonial Militia. Have you been there recently?"

"Maybe, why all the questions?"

"Well, I'm starting to think we might have some friends in common. What are your thoughts on the military peace keepers on Prime?"

For a second Teresa almost argued with him, her face betrayed her though. It was obvious she disagreed and try as she might she couldn't disguise her anger.

"I see, so you're no great lover of our vaunted friends in the Confederate Military," he said as he started to relax.

Teresa took a breath, she may have messed up but it had worked to her advantage. She had given the impression she had feelings, strong feelings about those on Prime, it wasn't her fault he had misread her emotions.

"The occupation on Avagana is good for business if that's what you're asking," she decided to add.

"I think we both know you want those supplies for the rebels on Prime. Many would call that treason. Perhaps I should mention this to our friends in the Confederate Navy?" he added with a mischievous smile.

Teresa was now starting to enjoy this, their conversation had moved on to an almost flirting position as Antonius became a little less suspicious of her. She twisted slightly, knowing it gave him a better view of the gap in her jacket and down to her breasts. She immediately spotted his eyes moving.

"Your friends! You really want those Navy assholes wandering around the station? I have an empty ship, you're the ones with supplies and the dodgy goods."

Teresa looked about and then leaned forward.

"I'll tell you what. I have a few more meetings to make, I know a man who might be able to help with your shipment. If you play your cards right you might even get a permanent arrangement out of it," he said.

"Sounds good, we'll be at the bar when he's ready to talk."

"If he's ready to talk, I think you mean."

Teresa stood up and grabbed the datapad, tucking it inside the leather pouch carried by Bishop.

"Whatever you say," she said dismissively.

Teresa moved to the doorway, her crewmates moving aside for her but still keeping a watchful eye over Antonius. As she reached the door she turned back just for a moment, smiling.

"Don't take too long, my customers don't have much time, if you know what I mean."

She turned and left the room, closely followed by the others. Rather than stopping she continued walking along the wide walkway, gazing at the stalls as they moved. Once they were out of earshot Bishop spoke quietly.

"Are we in?"

"Maybe, he obviously thinks we are running supplies through the blockade. The question is, will he talk to anyone higher up and if he does, will that get us the leads we need to crack this thing wide open?"

They moved past a few more stalls until reaching a pair of well-worn wooden doors. A drunk staggered out and crashed into Kowalski. Bishop grabbed the man and pushed him on his way.

"I guess this is the bar then?" he said with a laugh.

"Come on, we have some waiting to do," said Teresa.

Inside they found a long wooden bar with a tattooed man serving drinks. Half a dozen men and two women sat at tables drinking and on the wall an antiquated video display showed video feeds of events on Kerberos. Teresa plonked herself down on a barstool. The rest of her crew spread out with Barca and Williams heading for the pool table at the rear. The barman looked up.

"You're not from around here?"

"Quite. Whisky," she said sarcastically.

As the drink arrived a weasel-looking man entered the bar and looked about. As soon as he spotted Teresa he slunk over and dropped down next to her. The man lifted his hand and the barman wandered over, putting a drink in front of him, but saying nothing. The man took a swig and then turned to Teresa.

"Vasili, Antonius says you are involved in supplying the rebels."

Teresa threw back the whisky and instantly regretted it, but at least it helped calm her already frayed nerves.

"Really? He says a lot doesn't he?" she laughed.

The man looked around the room, checking for any problems before leaning in closer. He smelt like cinnamon but where he would have got that smell she had no idea.

"Look, we have a few interested parties on the station. This regime is going down and fast. There are going to be opportunities people with the contacts and the knowhow. You interested in upping the stakes and making some real money?"

Teresa looked over to Bishop who was busy watching them from a discreet distance.

"Hey, Bish, you interested in a bit more money?"

"Always," he came over and sat next to the man. "What do you have in mind?"

"Is it true, you have access to military grade blueprints?"

Teresa waved over to Kowalski who was now holding the satchel containing the encrypted military datapad. He pulled out the device and handed it to her. Before she switched it on she looked at the man for a moment before sliding the switch and turning it on. The first image to pop up was a technical schematic for the CES armour suits.

"Fuck, is that what I think it is?"

"Well, it ain't no pizza oven," said Bishop.

The man looked at the details, soaking in the facts and figures.

"Hey, this doesn't come cheap, we paid a heavy price for this information," Teresa said as she pulled back the datapad.

"That armour is the stuff I've heard about on Avagana. Those fascist bastards used it to kill civilians, you know that right?" he asked vehemently.

"Yeah, yeah, I know what they used it for. Now, what did you have in mind?" she asked.

"Well, there are some people here that could do with this kind of intel. To the right person I reckon we could make some serious money, I mean serious," he inched closer.

"We?" asked Bishop.

"I can get you a meeting with one of the groups from Avagana. You need to be quick, they won't be here for much longer, there's a price though."

"How much?" asked Teresa as she glanced at Bishop who was already placing a bug in the man's clothes.

"If I arrange a deal I want a fifty percent stake."

"Fifty percent, fuck off!" Bishop shouted who then turned away, feigning anger.

"Come on, we have things to do," Teresa stood up and dropped some cash on the bar for the bartender.

"Okay, easy now. Forty percent plus a look at the files," he countered.

Teresa turned towards him a little closer so that her skin was almost touching his face.

"I'll give you forty percent if you can arrange a meeting within the hour!"

"An hour? No way can I do something that fast!"

"Look, we have arrangements with another supplier, you make your arrangements or we move on. I don't have the time to mess about, it's up to you," she made to leave.

"Hey, how do I contact you?"

"My ship, the Tamarisk, don't leave it too long though." Then they were gone.

As they went down the corridor Teresa started to speed

up. Bishop was alongside, sensing something was wrong. He was about to speak when she pulled over to the side and retched, vomiting onto the metal floor. As Bishop held her, Barca approached.

"I've got a message from Anderson, he says he's picking up traffic from one of the bars two floors up. According to the station plans it's unused."

Teresa wiped her face and coughed a little before speaking. "Show me."

Barca passed the moving map to Teresa and she tracked the bug's movement and the new location.

"That has to be the place. Tell Anderson we're going in, he needs to have the ship ready in case we need to leave in a hurry."

Back in the main hallway they moved further along until they reached the door that led to different levels. Bishop went in first, closely followed by the rest of them. Teresa was last in and she quietly pulled the door behind her. The stairwell was dark and obviously little used. As they waited Williams checked his scanner for a better way to reach the area.

"The stairwell is blocked one level up. I've got a ventilated shaft running two metres outside the bar. Close enough for the UAVs?"

"It'll have to do. Come on, get them in position, I need to speak with Anderson." Teresa pulled out her radio.

"Anderson, we're in position. We're sending in the

UAVs now, are you tracking the bug?"

"He's entered the area now, send in the bugs. Once they are in position, get back to the ship."

Williams knelt down and took out a plastic box, laying it out on the floor. He opened the lid carefully to reveal four small metallic objects, each one the size of a finger. He looked up at Teresa who quickly gave him the nod. He took the first object out, twisted the cap and then placed it on the ground. Almost as soon as his hand was clear a wafer thin membrane extended from its side and then started to gently buzz. It rocked to the side and then took off hovering at head height. He quickly did the same to the rest of the units and in seconds all four were hovering near them.

"Okay, they are set to take the air ducts to the floor and then spread out. We need to wait until they reach whatever is going on. Everybody watch the door and stairs, if anybody comes in put them on the ground and shut them up," Teresa ordered.

* * *

Inside the Tamarisk Commander Anderson and Special Agent Johnson were busy watching the display panels. An additional screen showed a schematic of the station. Flashing dots showed the position of Teresa, her team and the bugged man. The first four screens all showed very dark images as the four miniature-robotic spies made their way to wherever the bugged man was heading.

"What do you think they'll find?" asked the Commander.

"Well, based on the intel we've received so far, I would guess anything from weapons and arms dealers for the insurgents, right up to a meeting between officials. We'll just have to wait and see."

On the schematic a number of blue dots started to move about the station.

"What are those?" asked Anderson.

"That isn't good, the security system monitors the private security firms protecting the different organisations at the station. Something has spooked them. Look, they're making their way to the stairwell."

"Shit, they must have rigged them with sensors!" Anderson grabbed the intercom system.

"Private Morato, we've got incoming, two security groups moving in on your position. I recommend you get into the main aisle and make your way slowly to the ship."

"Sir, the UAVs are not in place yet. If we leave we will not be able to send them new commands."

"They have their location data, let's just hope it's the right place. That isn't a suggestion, Morato, it's an order, now get your people out!"

"Yes, Commander."

He then looked back at the schematic, noting that the security teams went directly past Teresa and her group and towards one of the bars. It looked like it must have been a false alarm, or perhaps there was some unrelated incident. He looked back at the other four feeds and noted the first aerial vehicle was making its way through a narrow tunnel and to the air filter near the old club. On the video stream he could make out the grating in front of the robot but nothing the other side. With the poor light it was hard to tell if that was down to dirt or it was simply empty. He turned to the second robot and was surprised to see a clear view into a large room packed with dozens of people.

"Holy shit, are you getting this?" shouted the Commander.

"Already recording the data, Sir. Look, do you recognise Colonel Tyrol of the Agora Militia?"

"The bastard, he must be working with them!"

They were stood in a loose group around a central figure who wore thick robes that covered his entire body, leaving just a hint of his beard showing. The rest of the room was dark but the movement of shadows suggested there were more people along the perimeter.

"We are at a critical stage in the operation. Send a team and secure the ship, we'll take the data and dispose of her crew," said one man.

"I agree, it is too risky to involve anybody else, bring Antonius to us, we will have to explain to him why we do not allow strangers within our midst," spoke another.

The man in the middle of the room lifted up his hands,

indicating he wanted them all to be quiet.

"As you know, the struggle on Prime has expended our first wave of soldiers. More are being converted at our sites throughout the sector but we must have more time. With Kerberos out of the picture we can pick off each of the Confederate Colonies one at a time. In less than a month there will be enough converts to unleash against any single colony with a guarantee of victory."

A cheer echoed through the chamber, the volume forced the robot to reduce the recording level to avoid excessive noise.

"Now, our plan is already in motion, in the next hour you will see a demonstration of the Church's power and with it the dawn of the Union."

Commander Anderson pressed a few buttons to zoom the video feed in so he could get a better view of the meeting. As he moved in he noticed something familiar about the man in the robe. He moved in closer and took a still image from the feed, connecting it to the vessel's copy of the security database. It quickly found a match.

"Holy shit, that's the Bishop of Yama! I thought he was on Kerberos for the protests."

"Are you sure it's him?" asked Special Agent Johnson, who looked again. "It is him, but that's a holographic display, see it's flickering. He's not actually on the station!"

Anderson pointed at the data on the screen in front of him. As he looked he noticed the expression on Johnson's face.

"What is it?"

"President West, they're going to launch a coup, listen!"

He turned up the audio on the feed coming from the second robotic device. They listened to the details before Commander Anderson turned it down. He reached out and pressed a few keys to combine the data into a compressed packet for transmission. It only took a few seconds before it was ready. The communications relay was automatically tracking the correct destination point in case they needed to send data back in a hurry. He hit the key to find it immediately blocked.

"They know!" Johnson pointed at the screen.

A number of men ran in with scanners and one appeared in front of the second UAV before the video feed cut out.

"The signal is blocked, we need to get out of Dodge!" said Anderson as he rushed to the cockpit and strapped himself in.

As he began the start up procedure Agent Johnson shouted back along the corridor to the Commander.

"They're eight metres away and moving slowly, they must be trying to leave discreetly."

Anderson pulled the intercom from the ceiling of the craft so he could speak directly with the team.

"Morato! Blackwatch! Get your ass here and fast, we've got serious problems!"

* * *

Spartan sat in the anteroom alongside Marcus. They had been there for over two hours as an emergency session was being held between President West and his security council. The announcements of the colonial secession were spreading like wildfire on every single media outlet. From where they were positioned they could easily hear the shouting and chanting outside the building as large numbers of the public had congregated to protest against the Confederacy or against the breaking up of the old institution. Every few minutes the sound of police sirens and vehicles indicated yet more incidents between the groups as they argued and sometimes fought outside the building.

Marcus leaned over, speaking quietly. "What do you think is going to happen here?"

"What do you mean?" replied Spartan, not entirely sure which problem he was referring too.

"Kerberos, do you think they will secede as well? Just listen to them out there. I reckon they'll lynch him either way."

"No, have you seen President West? He looks like a diehard Confederate to me, but I don't think he's the problem though. You saw the video feeds. There are plenty of people that want him and us out. In my experience people often want change just for the sake of it."

The two men were silent, Spartan listened to the sounds outside as he looked at his datapad to check the media feeds. Every channel was showing the same, the protests and violence in the streets outside.

"Look at them," Spartan showed the device to Marcus.

"As soon as West tells them the official line there is going to be uproar, I guarantee it," said Marcus.

"You're probably right. With most of the colonies of Prime, Orthrus and Agora already gone, if Kerberos leaves as well what will happen with the Fleet? What will happen to us?"

A loud chorus of shouting and chanting could be heard though the walls.

"Listen to them, can you believe the fuss they're making out there?"

"I don't know, that sounded like it was inside the building to me," said Spartan as he look around. The Marine Guards seemed unperturbed by the sounds. Spartan approached the two guards waiting at the bottom of the wide grand staircase that led to the visitor apartments. He could see the two men were talking to each other. As soon as they spotted him they stopped and the nearest turned to him.

"Everything okay, Sergeant?"

"Yeah, did hear noise inside the building?"

"It's okay, there was an attempt to break the perimeter wall on the North side. We've already cleared the area and arrested the hooligans. Just a few broken windows," he said reassuringly.

Spartan turned to move back. He wasn't sure though, something wasn't right and right now he couldn't put his finger on it.

* * *

Teresa was first up the ramp and inside the ship. Once safe she moved to the side and turned back to watch the rest of her team join her. Bishop was next and closely followed by the other three. Only Williams was left when the guards appeared. A blast of gunfire erupted and clattered against the metal body of the ship. Two rounds struck Williams, one in the leg and the other in the stomach. A spray of bright blood splattered forward and onto the ramp. He collapsed to the ground as the others jumped to safety.

"Get him in!" Teresa shouted as she pulled out her pistol and squeezed off a dozen rounds in quick succession.

The guards ducked into cover, trying to avoid the barrage of fire from the pistol. Bishop and Barca pulled carbines from the weapons' mount near the top of the ramp and proceeded to fire short bursts. The guards, now taken by surprise with their accuracy and firepower, started to retreat. Kowalski rushed down the ramp, a bullet impacting just a metre from him as he grabbed Williams by the arm. He started to drag his lifeless body along the ramp. As he moved a long, slick pattern of blood ran down the metal, it didn't look good.

"Get in, we need to move!" Anderson ordered over the speakers fitted throughout the ship.

More rounds rattled around the bodywork of the spacecraft and Barca had to drop his carbine so that he could come out and help drag Williams inside.

"Bishop, keep their heads down!" shouted Teresa.

She grabbed another carbine from the weapons' rack and then dropped to her knees, aiming at the guards who were still returning fire. As she was about to pull the trigger one of the men stood up and fired a short burst that missed by just a fraction.

"Bastard!" she cried and in one quick motion, she selected the range finder and launched a large calibre explosive round in the man's direction. As it rushed past the cover used by the guards it armed itself, then exploded in a small flash. The impact blasted the two men, one was already killed by the blast and the other smoked from the heat. The man tried to move back to safety but Teresa sent another round into his chest. It sent him flying through the air, killing him instantly.

With the fight temporarily over Teresa reached down and helped them drag Williams inside. She hit the seal button to force the door shut. As it slammed into position she could still hear the sound of small arms fire bouncing off the vessel. She looked down at Williams but he was already dead. His eyes were lifeless and she saw the hole in his chest. She lifted her hand to her face, angry with the guards and with herself, for losing one of their team.

"Get strapped in, we're out of here!" Anderson shouted over the speakers.

Bishop had already secured the body and was strapping himself in at the communications console. Teresa strapped in next to him. Agent Johnson was still trying to isolate the source of the jamming so they could send their signal. Before Teresa could speak a great clunking sound indicated they were clear of the station. The rumble from the engines started up and the familiar feeling in her stomach of the change in G forces returned. For just a second she thought she might throw up but calmed down at the last moment.

"I'm still trying, but they must have sensors fitted amongst the asteroids out here to create an area-wide signal dampening field. It will be three minutes, maybe four before we can send a signal."

Commander Anderson, who was still in the cockpit, assisted the autopilot in working on the most direct route out of the Rim. The ship was already building up speed, but in this treacherous part of space they were unable to accelerate to the maximum. The short corridor joining the communication panel and the cockpit was only six metres long. Teresa could see Commander Anderson from where she sat.

"Bishop, get the weapon system ready, I think we might

have company!"

Teresa looked at the navigation screen, quickly picking up a number of merchant vessels and at least one gunboat that was moving into position to intercept them.

"How are we going to get past them?" she asked. "They'll just destroy us from long distance before we can escape!"

Johnson smiled at her as he started sending ghost signals to some of the approaching ships, making it more difficult for them to track and lock on their ship.

"This ship has more than a few surprises. Get to the communications array, we'll be in the clear for transmission shortly."

"Brace for impact, we have two gunboats on a strafing run!" shouted Anderson, his voice bouncing through the crew sections of the ship.

Before they had time to respond, the clatter of canon rounds thudded through the forward section. Incredibly none of the rounds were able to cause any significant damage but to the casual observer the exterior of the ship did sustain carbon scoring and fractures to some of the fake metal skin.

* * *

Spartan and Marcus were still watching the video feeds of the protests when a direct communication announcement came on Spartan's datapad automatically closing the media feeds. The outer rim of his device glowed red, he hadn't even seen this before.

"What the hell is that?" asked Marcus, instantly suspicious.

Spartan lifted up the pad to see a request for a cipher to decode a classified message that had been repeated and bumped down from the orbiting CCS Santa Cruz. He checked the sender before pressing anything and noted it was anonymous, at least that's what it said. For a moment he considered doing nothing but there was a good chance it was important and the fact it came from the ship must mean it had some kind of providence.

"Screw it!" he said and quickly input his cipher codes.

The display flashed and turned to an image of a bloodied Teresa.

"Teresa!" said Spartan, a little louder than he intended.

Marcus moved over, looking at the video. "What has she got into now?"

The video was a one-way transmission and sent some time ago due to the time difference between locations in the sector.

"This is Private Morato of the Confederate Marine Corps," she started before the video feed crackled and started to phase shift.

In the background a number of people were rushing about and sparks and flashes suggested there was some kind of ongoing violence or emergency. As the picture settled Teresa reappeared and continued.

"Our mission to the Rim has revealed a plot centred on Typhon, leader of the..." the image disappeared and the audio crackled for several seconds again, "intend to assassinate President West..." the audio dropped out again.

"A coup? What the hell!" Marcus looked around, seeing nothing out of the ordinary.

"Guards Company...assassinate President...church" the audio finally cut out completely.

For a short while the video feed continued, Spartan tried as hard as he could but he couldn't work out what she was saying. He could however make out the background was the bulkhead section of a ship of some kind. It wasn't military, or at least not like any ship he had been on yet. Then the image cut as suddenly as it had started to be replaced with a message indicating it was the end of the transmission. Spartan was stunned. It might have been the image of Teresa, or more likely the message, but for the briefest of moments he was paralysed with the arrival of the information.

"Spartan? Come on, what's the plan?" asked an anxious Marcus.

It was as though a switch had been flicked inside Spartan's brain as he suddenly started to glance around the anteroom and at the Marine Guards stationed at all the key locations.

"I tell you what we're going to do, we're going to get the General and the President out of here!" he said as quietly as he could.

"How though? If the Guards are in on the plan then what friends do we have left?"

"Shit, you've got a point, come on!"

The two turned to the door that led to where the meeting with President West and his Cabinet was taking place. Spartan placed his hand on the door and turned the handle, nothing happened. He pushed the door and still it remained firmly shut.

"Hey, what are you doing?" said one of the Marine Guards as he approached.

"We need to get inside!"

The marine raised his carbine and pointed it at Spartan, as he did so the other five Marine Guards in the open room did the same.

"Oh man, this is bullshit!" swore Marcus.

Spartan put his hands out in front in a gesture of compliance and moved slowly towards the man.

"We just need to speak with the President, something has come up," said Spartan again, this time even firmer in his tone.

"I don't care what you want, he is being taken care of, you just stay here and keep out of..." he didn't get to finish as Spartan ducked to the side and jumped in, grabbing the carbine. He swung it around to strike the man in the head.

The guard slumped to the floor as Spartan lowered the weapon, pointing it at the rest of the marines.

"Get it open!" Spartan shouted to Marcus who was already kicking the door to try and open it. Finally becoming frustrated he pulled out his sidearm and emptied three rounds into the frame before it finally buckled.

"Go!" Spartan shouted and with all the speed they could muster the two rushed inside.

As Spartan emerged into the room he was shocked to find it deserted. Not a single member of the Cabinet or even the President was there. The two spread out, looking for any signs of the men in the large meeting room. A shape appeared at the door and Spartan put two rounds into the open space, discouraging anybody from entering for now.

"They won't wait long, we need to find them!" Marcus said as he looked behind each of the desks and chairs.

Another man approached the doorway and this time he entered the room. Spartan did his best to not kill the man and put a round into his upper leg, the man dropped, crying out in pain.

"Here!" Marcus called out as he found a false wall at the back of the room. With a tug he pulled it open to reveal several bodies slumped across the desks. In the middle of the room lay the bloodied body of President West as well as three Marine Guards.

"Oh shit, Marcus, it's a setup!"

They ducked into the second room and took cover among the already shattered decks and tables. As they waited it was evident a terrible scene of violence had taken place in the last hour. Marcus checked the President for a pulse before turning back to Spartan.

"He's cold, they must have done this just after they went in, how did we not hear it?"

Part of the wall to the side turned white and they were knocked backwards by the violent blast. As Spartan tried to get up four men in black body armour of the Guards Unit formed a line. Each of them was pointing a thermal shotgun at him. Spartan shook his head, trying to clear the fuzziness from the stun grenade. He looked to his right, Marcus was unconscious and slumped across a desk.

"You bastards!"

He started to lift his weapon when General Rivers entered the room. For a second Spartan thought he might be behind the assassination but then he saw the cuffs on his wrists and the gag on his face. Two more armoured guards flanked him. As Spartan watched in shock the men rushed forward to secure him. With his instincts kicking in he emptied the pistol into the first but the pistol wasn't powerful enough to penetrate the thick armour and they were instantly on top of him. He punched and kicked with all his strength but there were too many. In just under a minute they had him knocked to the ground and unconscious.

* * *

Admiral Jarvis stood in the CiC of the CCS Wasp, waiting for news from Commander Anderson. In the last ten minutes a number of jammed data packets had been received but there was too much corruption for her people to obtain much solid information. She was starting to become impatient.

"Captain, any news from the Fleet at Kerberos?"

Captain Hardy spoke briefly with the Communications Officer before turning back to her.

"Nothing, Admiral, the last update was the regular sitrep one hour ago."

She stood, examining the disposition of the ships on her display. Already a number of vessels were heading to Kerberos and Prime to reinforce the ships already there.

"Put me through to the Crusader, they must have heard something by now!" she said, her patience finally running out.

"Sir," the Captain gave the orders to his crew.

The officers moved about, realigning their communication arrays to receive the narrowband encrypted data channels. There was something wrong, Admiral Jarvis could tell by the crew's body language that they were having problems.

"What is it?" she asked finally.

"All channels to Kerberos are being jammed, Admiral,"

replied the Communications Officer.

"Jammed, by whom?"

"I...uh...don't know, Sir. The signal is being overlaid with an unencrypted video stream, it is being played out on all frequencies."

"Put it on," ordered Captain Hardy.

"The main display slid away from the strategic map and to a standard definition colour video stream of a podium behind which hung the banners of the Church of Echidna.

"What is this nonsense?" she demanded.

There was no time to answer her as a man in a robe stepped up to the podium and removed his hood.

"I, Typhon, Bishop of Yama City and head of our good Church and the people of Kerberos welcome all with open hands. I thank you," he said as he lifted his hands.

Admiral Jarvis turned her head in disbelief at the platform being used by this man.

"Fellow Kerberons and citizens of Proxima. I have been asked to speak by the Vice President of Kerberos. Within the last few hours a terrible event has occurred. Not content with violence and depravity on Prime, the agents of the Confederacy have struck in this very city. President West and a number of his key advisors have been assassinated by a well organised and savage assault by agents of the Confederate Navy," he said as he waved to someone off camera.

Six men in black armour appeared and dragged the

bloodied and bruised shapes of General Rivers, Spartan and Marcus into view.

"God no!" exclaimed Admiral Jarvis.

"These men are responsible for this terrible crime and they will be sent to an undisclosed location where they will await their trial. Even more incredible is that the operation was under the direct command of General Rivers, one of the senior Confederate Commanders in Proxima!"

The guards dragged the prisoners out of the view of the camera so that the Bishop was the only person remaining in shot.

"Due to these terrible events the Vice President has chosen to remain hidden until our security forces can guarantee his safety. His first order however is to establish the Church as a moral oversight to his administration. Though a terrible night, this change in policy to the atheist and abhorrent regime of the past should gives us cause for joy. For decades our good people have slaved under the tyranny of big business. Workers earn little, yet work longer and harder as the rich become richer. Human morality has become shameful with even our own leaders living in shame and decadence. Today the partnership between the government of Kerberos and the Church announces its intention to help any colony to become a safe and prosperous place to live outside of the greedy paws of the Confederacy. No more will our citizens be forced to fight wars on foreign lands for an oppressive regime."

He paused, waiting as if there was a momentous addition to his speech. The silence extends to almost ten seconds before he continued.

"How many of our colonial brothers have been forced to join the military? Some because of debts to oppressive companies, others for so-called crimes against the state. This duty of service and war is a crime against humanity and we have been working tirelessly for the last five years on the creation of an alternative to this service. Our loyal citizens should never have to fight in another war or die in another battle. I am therefore proud to announce the wonder that is the Biomech. A biological machine that will provide our people with safety and security, while removing the risk of war to our citizens," he said with a gleam in his eye.

From the right hand side of the camera stepped two of the shock troopers. They seemed almost identical the ones that had fought on Prime. They looked like normal people, just bigger and more substantial. They both wore a minimalist level of armour, much like the tight fitting PDS suits of the marines. Their heads were covered with metal masks that conveniently covered their mutated muscles and jaws. In perfect synchronisation the two warriors dropped to one knee and bowed to the camera. As they remained totally still, a man in the robes of the Zealots approached the Bishop and spoke quietly before turning and moving out of view. The Bishop then looked up and smiled at the camera.

"We have received word following the discussions between the Chief Ministers of Kerberos and those of the Colonies of Prime, Orthrus and Agora. They have all announced their intention to secede from the oppressive capitalist regime of the Confederacy. I call on all military forces to join us and return Proxima to the people. From today, any city or colony joining our union of peace and brotherhood will be provided full protection against military intervention, piracy and organised crime through the deployment of our loyal Biomechs," he signalled to both shock troopers who then stood and left.

"Peace to you all," said Typhon as he placed his hand on his heart.

The video feed cut off abruptly. Admiral Jarvis continued staring at the video display in disbelief. She had sent General Rivers as a representative and now the situation in Prime seemed to pale in insignificance to this new threat in the sector.

"The jamming has stopped, Admiral," said the Communications Officer.

Captain Hardy approached the Admiral, standing in front and looking for a moment as though he was going to draw a weapon. Instead he pulled out a datapad, he pressed one button and handed it to her.

"While the feed was coming in we managed to decode

some of the data coming from the Rim. It is Commander Anderson and he says he has information on the coup on Kerberos."

Admiral Jarvis looked down at the datapad, checking the details for herself. When she finished reading she moved back to her strategic map and reached out, touching each of the seceding colonies and tapping them. The colours of the sites turned grey until little remained in the System that appeared loyal to the Confederacy.

"What are your orders, Admiral?"

Admiral Jarvis stood silent, looking at the map as if she expected some great solution to present itself. It wasn't to be though. She turned to the Captain.

"We will stop this before it can spread," she said firmly.

Moving across the CiC she reached the communication array.

"Record this message and send it out to every combat unit in the sector!"

The officer sitting at his desk looked quickly at Captain Hardy who immediately gave him the nod. He pressed a few buttons and then handed the microphone to the Admiral.

"This is Admiral Jarvis, Supreme Commander of all Confederation Units in Proxima. A military coup has been staged on Kerberos by terrorist forces. I am placing all Units on maximum alert! All personnel are to report to their stations. Any attempts to enter Confederation facilities will be responded to with lethal force."

She paused, realising the decision she was making could have catastrophic consequences for the region.

"As the legal representative of the Confederacy, I declare any acts of secession to be illegal and against the articles of the Confederacy agreed to by every colony in this sector. Any attempts to break the articles will be met by the full force of the Confederate Military!" she said and then slammed down the intercom.

The entire room was silent, the officers either waiting to hear what she had to say next or just waiting for their orders. Admiral Jarvis turned back to examine the display and the ever shrinking influence of the Confederacy. As she looked at the screen she called over to the Communications Officer.

"Get me through to Commander Anderson, we need information!"

"Aye, Sir," said the man as he proceeded to try and link directly to the Tamarisk.

"This is it then?" asked Captain Hardy, his face showing obvious horror at the situation.

"No, it isn't. We are facing the greatest threat since the Great War," she said sternly.

"War? We're already fighting a war, Sir," said the Captain.

Admiral Jarvis turned back to him, her eyes burning with anger at the situation.

"This war hasn't even begun!"

CPSIA information can be obtained at www.ICGtesting.com
Printed in the USA
LVOW062101311012

305187LV00004B/38/P

9 781906 512309